"We had lots of dreams and plans back then," he said as he eased the Range Rover up the ramp of the parking garage. **"The two of us were going to set the world on fire."**

"In the end, we only burned each other."

"It wasn't that bad," said Ian. "Was it?"

"We broke up and haven't spoken for more than two years. So, I'd say it wasn't good."

Ian edged into a parking space marked as reserved. "No regrets for moving on, then?"

"Regrets," she echoed with a short laugh. "I've never loved anyone in my life the way I love you."

"Loved?" he asked. "Or love?"

Petra's breath caught ██████ fool to rush to Ian.

It wasn't simply that sh███ was well equipped to h████████████ back what she had lost—███████████████.

His question still hung in the air, like a cartoon speech bubble with a trail of dots. *Loved or love?*

* * *

Rocky Mountain Justice: These Colorado mercenaries fight for duty and honor

* * *

If you're on Twitter, tell us what you think of Harlequin Romantic Suspense! #harlequinromsuspense

Dear Reader,

Like the old saying goes, it takes a village to raise a child. And if that's true, then it takes a small city to get a book into production. With that in mind, I need to thank several people who helped get *Rocky Mountain Valor* into the world.

To Susan, my editor: thanks for your support, guidance and never-ending optimism. Thanks also to Patience, the senior editor of the line, for your leadership and vision. The art department has created some amazing covers that have left me breathless. Thanks also to my agent for believing in me. I wouldn't be here without you, Chris. I also want to thank all my writer friends and girlfriends for their support over the years, with a special shout-out to Michaela Stoughton. We might not solve all the world's problems, but thank you for helping me create the best story possible. Finally, to my family. You are my world. Full stop.

I have one final thank-you to you, dear reader! I am proud, honored and humbled that you've taken time from your busy life to read *Rocky Mountain Valor*.

Enjoy!

Jennifer D. Bokal

PS: Check out my new website, jenbokal.com.

ROCKY MOUNTAIN VALOR

Jennifer D. Bokal

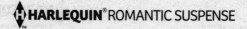

H HARLEQUIN® ROMANTIC SUSPENSE

Recycling programs
for this product may
not exist in your area.

ISBN-13: 978-1-335-45657-1

Rocky Mountain Valor

Copyright © 2018 by Jennifer D. Bokal

Printed in U.S.A.

www.Harlequin.com

Jennifer D. Bokal is the author of the bestselling ancient-world historical romance *The Gladiator's Mistress* and the second book in the Champions of Rome series, *The Gladiator's Temptation*. Happily married to her own alpha male for twenty years, she enjoys writing stories that explore the wonders of love in many genres. Jen and her husband live in upstate New York with their three beautiful daughters, two aloof cats and two very spoiled dogs.

Books by Jennifer D. Bokal

Harlequin Romantic Suspense

Rocky Mountain Justice

Her Rocky Mountain Hero
Her Rocky Mountain Defender
Rocky Mountain Valor

Visit the Author Profile page
at Harlequin.com for more titles.

To John. You are my always and forever.

Prologue

Denver, Colorado
5:30 a.m.
August 21

Ian Wallace pressed his back into the wall and drew his semiautomatic pistol. The visor of his helmet was pulled low. Black pants. Black shirt. Black Kevlar vest. He blended into the darkness like a shadow.

"Ready," he said, his voice pitched low. His helmet mic transmitted his command to his team of ten, waiting behind him. His words also went to a van, parked three blocks away, that served as a mobile headquarters.

There was a singular objective with the raid—arrest the three drug dealers, dubbed Comrades One, Two and Three. Yet he was far more interested in what the trio of Comrades knew about Nikolai Mateev, the godfather of Russian organized crime.

For Ian, the hunt for Nikolai Mateev was more than a job, it was his life's work. It covered his skin, raced through his veins and filled his lungs. He hadn't felt this soul-deep yearning in years. And the memory of the last time stung deeply. Not for the first time, he found the image of Petra Sloane stealing into his mind at the most inconvenient moment.

He shook his head to clear it, determined to free himself of all thoughts of her. Past was past. They were over. The most important bust of his career—of his life—was about to go down, and he had to remain focused. Eternity passed in the span of a single heartbeat.

"Go! Go! Go!" he said out loud.

Two agents rushed forward, swinging a battering ram, breaking the lock and knocking the door off its hinges. Ian lobbed a flash-bang grenade into the room. Turning away, he ducked down. Light and sound exploded as tendrils of smoke wafted over him.

Comrade Three lay on the floor. A seam had been sliced into his forehead and it filled with bright red blood. Flex-cuffs were immediately slipped around the man's wrists, and two team members remained as guards. The rest fanned out. Three went upstairs. Ian, with the remaining three, searched the ground floor.

Voices drew Ian's attention. He sprinted down a short hallway to the rear of the house. He entered the kitchen in time to see Comrade One slip through the back door and into the predawn mist. Comrade Two rushed after him.

"You aren't going anywhere." Grabbing him by the shoulder, Ian gave a hard pull, throwing the man to the floor. Instantly, three guns were pointed at his head. The Russian lifted his hands in surrender.

Pulse and breath resonating inside his helmet, Ian ran out the back door in time to watch Comrade One scuttle over the fence. He stopped the chase, his eyes drawn to the ground. The final member of the team writhed in pain, a knife protruding from his thigh.

Ian slid his gun into a holster at his hip as he dropped to the ground and began to apply pressure to the wound.

"What happened?" he asked, his attention torn between his injured teammate and the escaped Russian gangster.

The other man gritted his teeth. "It was Comrade One. I didn't see the knife and he stabbed me when I tried to apprehend him. I'm sorry, man. I screwed up."

It was a serious mistake, for certain. Yet there was nothing to be gained with second-guesses.

"We'll get you patched up," said Ian. Then into his mic, "Man down. I need backup, stat."

Roman DeMarco, an RMJ employee with combat experience, slid in next to the downed man. He began to administer rudimentary first aid. "I've got this," he said. "Go."

Ian was already consumed with the need to capture Comrade One. He took off at a sprint and vaulted over the wooden fence.

He landed in a neighboring yard. It was empty and eerily quiet. Ian scanned his surroundings. Nothing. Yet he refused to give up so easily.

With a curse, he jumped over the next fence, dashed through the yard and jumped over the next two fences after that. Landing on a sidewalk, he spun toward the sounds of screeching tires, as a set of headlights raced up the street. The car swerved. The undercarriage hit the curb as the bumper headed straight for him.

Without time to think, Ian propelled himself up. He came down hard, landing on the hood. His shoulder slammed into the windshield and he pitched forward. In that split second, he caught a glimpse of the driver. Comrade One. Ian continued the roll, landing on the ground. The acrid smell of burned rubber filled the air as the car dropped off the curb, a shower of sparks trailing behind when it sped off into the brightening morning.

Frustration from this latest setback filled his gut. He got to his feet, and for the folks in the HQ van, said, "Yuri Kuzntov, Comrade One, has gotten away. Repeat, Kuzntov, Comrade One, has fled via a dark gray sedan, partial Colorado license plates Foxtrot Echo Four Nine. I'm returning to the scene."

"Copy that" came the reply.

Lights atop police cruisers, strobing red and white, were visible from four blocks away, while the wail of sirens grew closer. The front door, knocked off its hinges, had been set aside on the stoop. Ian crossed the threshold and removed his helmet, tucking it under his arm.

Comrade Three sat on the sofa, a medic treating his minor head wound with an antiseptic wipe. With curly dark hair and a beard that didn't quite cover his chin, the Russian was the youngest of the group—aged twenty-four, Ian knew—and the least important.

Turning to the medic, he said, "Get DeMarco to talk to this one."

Roman DeMarco, Ian's first employee at Rocky Mountain Justice, was ex–Delta Force and fluent in half a dozen languages, including Russian. Ian spoke Russian as well, but his responsibility was to delegate and prioritize—whether he liked it or not.

"I'll get right on it," the medic said.

Ian nodded his thanks and moved to the kitchen. Four ashtrays, filled to overflowing, sat atop the table. Dirty dishes lay on the counter and a trash can vomited pizza boxes and takeout containers onto the sticky floor. Without question, these men had been living rough for days, perhaps weeks. Were they waiting for something? Or someone?

Ian hoped like hell that it was Nikolai Mateev.

Comrade Two sat in a kitchen chair with his hands cuffed together before him. He was the oldest member of the group. His hair was sparse, and his skin was like timeworn parchment—lined, slightly yellow and dry. Inked into his ring finger was an Orthodox cross with three bars. An outline of a diamond surrounded the whole. It was the initial tattoo for the *vory v zakone*, or thieves-in-law. Russian organized crime. Several other tattoos covered his hands and what could be seen of his wrists. One was for a prison where he'd served time. Another for a crime committed. The rest of his body would be the same and have a more complete list of his misdeeds than any dossier prepared by Ian's old colleagues at MI5.

Ian eyed him closely. *"Ty govorish' po-angliyski?" Do you speak English?* Even though Ian could have conversed in Russian, there were two other uniformed police standing guard, and he wanted to make sure they heard what was being said in case the conversation was ever part of a court case.

The man snorted. "Better than your Russian."

"Where's Nikolai?"

"I don't know anyone named Nikolai."

Ian refused to play games. "If you can't help me, comrade, I can't help you."

"I don't want your help."

"I can arrange for you to be housed in a minimum-security prison. Nice meals. Cable TV. Tennis courts."

"You think you can bribe me?"

"No," said Ian, "but I can make it look like you cooperated and are receiving favorable treatment. How long do you think Nikolai Mateev would let you live, even in prison, if he thought you'd talked to the authorities for an easier sentence? Or you can really talk, and I'll help you disappear."

The man nudged the sooty ashtray with a finger. It was a simple reaction, but Ian knew he'd hit a nerve.

"You with the FBI?"

Ian ignored the question. Let Comrade Two think what he wanted.

"You don't sound like an FBI agent. I bet you aren't. Not with that accent, anyway. You're English," he said. "I can tell."

Ian remained mute, unwilling to share even the most basic details of his life. Let the other man prattle and get nervous. It was just a matter of time before he'd talk. Leaning back in his seat, he prepared to wait the old Russian out.

"Ian?"

He looked at the person who had called his name. Another RMJ agent, Cody Samuels, stood in the doorway. During his years with the DEA, Cody had led dozens of searches like this and Ian was glad for his expertise.

Wearing the black tactical gear of all RMJ operatives, Cody had also donned a pair of blue latex gloves. He held a laptop computer. "I found this," he said, "hidden behind a wall."

Ian could feel it in his bones: the computer was going to be a critical link in the long chain that finally led to Mateev.

He turned to Comrade Two. "What's the password?"

"I don't know."

Ian didn't care if the old Russian was lying or not. "If you can't be any help, then I don't need you anymore." He waved to the two uniformed police officers. "Take him away."

"Wait," said Comrade Two. "That laptop was only

used for email. I never touched the computer, though, so I don't know what was sent or received."

"Take him away," Ian repeated to the cops. "But have him placed in solitary for now."

Comrade Two was lifted to his feet and ushered from the room.

Ian waited until everyone was gone and only he and Cody remained. He gestured to the computer. "Whatever we find will be important."

"I thought as much. Just wanted to let you know before I turned it over to Jones."

Special Agent Marcus Jones was with the FBI. At the beginning of the year, he had contracted Rocky Mountain Justice to find Nikolai Mateev. It had proved to be an uncomfortable relationship for Jones and Ian—neither man wholly a subordinate, nor entirely in charge.

Yet this was RMJ's raid. The computer was their find. But once Jones took over, Ian would never see the computer again.

And he damn well wasn't going to let that happen.

"For now, let's keep this discovery between the team. We don't know how significant it may turn out to be," Ian answered.

Cody narrowed his gaze. "This is evidence," he said, "and belongs with the FBI."

"That may be, but right now we have custody."

"I'm not going to get into a pissing match over evidence that we're lawfully bound to surrender."

Then again, maybe Cody had spent too long working in government bureaucracy. "Jones hired us to do the things that he can't, to circumvent the law. You know what will happen once he gets this computer. It'll be tagged as evidence then sent to the tech lab for analysis. It will be weeks, or maybe months, before anyone will act on what's found."

"And that's the law," said Cody.

Ian stared him down, refusing to yield. "If we have the laptop, we can get information now."

"By breaking the law?" said Cody. "We agreed to this mission. There are still protocols to follow."

"We aren't going to catch Nikolai Mateev by following all the rules," said Ian, his tone growing steely.

While with the DEA, Cody had opened a secret investigation against the Mateev crime family. An informant had been killed and it cost Cody his job—and his reputation at the agency. The road to getting his life back had been dangerous, including discovery of betrayal by people Cody had had true faith in…until Mateev and his money had undermined everything. Cody had nearly lost his life, and the woman and child he loved, fighting the Russian crime lord's influence.

"Point taken," he said now.

A rancid notion came to Ian. If he was really serious about stopping Nikolai Mateev, he'd have to break more than a few laws. He'd have to abandon every principle he'd ever possessed, break every oath he'd taken.

In fact, the only way to really stop Nikolai would be to put him in the grave.

Chapter 1

Petra Sloane sat in the cramped radio studio, her elbows resting on the table. A microphone on a metal arm was suspended before her eyes. A blue-and-orange banner hung on the wall, reading All Sports, All the Time. The tagline of Denver's sports station KDEN AM 1460.

An illuminated red off-air light glowed in the corner. The interviewer, Steve Chan, sat opposite Petra. He had a similar microphone and a reputation for being the toughest sportscaster on the Front Range. As a commercial for custom floor mats ended, Steve flicked up his fingers—one, two, three. The light in the corner changed from red to green and the words *On Air* appeared.

"Welcome back to our final segment of the morning," Steve said. "We have with us, in studio, Petra Sloane, a renowned sports agent who represents many famous names in the Denver scene, most notably Joe Owens, quarterback for the Colorado Mustangs. Petra, thanks for agreeing to sit in the Hot Seat today."

Petra could think of a thousand places she'd rather be than on the popular radio show, forced to talk about a client. The stress registered as a pain between her brows. Forcing herself to ignore the oncoming headache, she leaned in to the mic. "It's a real pleasure to be here, Steve," she lied.

Even though she was on the radio, Petra had taken extra care with her appearance that morning. She wore a sheath dress of ballet-slipper pink, with a matching lip gloss. The light color set off her tanned skin, just as the short sleeves accentuated her toned and muscled arms. Her dark wavy hair was up in a bun at the nape of her neck.

"Let's not waste any time," Steve began. "Your client has had a rough month. Two weeks ago, he was kicked out of a downtown club for disturbing the peace. Then last week there was a viral video of Joe cursing at a waitress who didn't get his order right. And just yesterday he was ejected from a press conference after throwing a punch at my fellow KDEN reporter for asking a question about the preseason debacle against Washington. The city of Denver loves Joe, but I have to ask—what's his deal?"

Petra exhaled. "There is no deal. I think we forget that sports stars, or any celebrities, are humans first. They have good days and bad, just like the rest of us.

I'm sure you've had difficult days, and said or done things you later regretted. Why isn't Joe Owens allowed the same latitude?"

"I've never screamed at a waitress for not remembering to bring ketchup with my meal," said Steve.

Petra's phone vibrated with an incoming text. It was her boss, Mike Dawson, with a terse two-word message: Take control.

"I'm glad to hear that you've never done anything so stupid," Petra said. "But I think we forget that celebrities are people whose lives are lived under a microscope. Joe's behavior has been bad, rotten really, but we all deserve a second chance."

"By now, Joe Owens is on to his third, fourth and fifth chances. When do we stop forgiving or demand better?"

Steve was right, and Petra refused to argue, despite what her boss wanted. The seconds ticked by. "Now," she said, finally. "We should require better now."

Steve lifted his eyebrows and cleared his throat. "I'm surprised to hear you be so honest."

Petra shrugged, then remembered that she was on the radio. "Everyone should be more forthright."

"Why do you do it, then?" Steve asked. "Why did you become a sports agent?"

Petra smiled and shook her head. "I didn't come here to talk about myself."

"I'm just asking because you're the first agent we've had on the show. My listeners will be interested in hearing about you and your job."

Fair enough. Besides, if she talked about herself,

then she didn't have to defend the indefensible any longer. "I played basketball in college and when I graduated, I wanted to remain involved with sports. Going to law school and becoming an agent seemed like the perfect way to achieve that. And it is, really. I help bring the players to the fans, and also help players manage their own careers, finances…you know, the works."

"Seems like the safe answer," said Steve.

"It's the truth," she said.

"Why do you really do it? The money? The parties? What is it?"

Petra flipped the phone in her hand. She was here to help Joe's reputation, not bare her soul. And yet she said, "My dad played for the American Hockey League and he did okay financially. And yes, he had an agent. One day, the agent is in Mexico with more than two million dollars that my father had earned over his career." She took a deep breath. "That situation taught me that I want to be a very different kind of agent. Someone who represents her clients on the field or the court, but who can also truly look after them when they need me. I want them to be able to trust me with everything."

"That's rough," said Steve. "I'm sorry about your dad."

"It gave me a unique perspective," she replied.

"Joe Owens is a lucky guy to have you for an agent. But I gotta ask one last question." Steve leaned forward. "There's always a scandal or two lurking. Like you said, famous people get their mistakes examined under a microscope." He exhaled. "Do you ever get sick of dealing with people like Joe?"

Setting the phone aside, she said, "It's all part of the job."

The green light in the corner began to flash. "That's all the time we have. Before I go, I'd like to thank Petra Sloane for sitting in the Hot Seat. Next up, the morning's headlines."

The red light proclaimed they were off the air. Steve leaned across the table and offered his palm to Petra. They shook hands. "Thanks for coming in. Now I wish your client had the courage to take his turn and explain himself."

"Maybe next time," she offered.

"Are you saying Joe's shenanigans will continue?"

Petra hadn't meant to imply anything, especially not to a media personality like Steve Chan. Her phone vibrated, shimmying across the table. As she glanced at the screen, she couldn't help but think of the old cliché of being saved by the bell. "That's my boss," she said. "I have to take this call."

"Go ahead," said Steve, "and thanks again."

Petra swiped the call open as she exited the studio. "Hey," she said.

"That's the sorriest excuse for an interview I've ever heard. Why didn't you defend Joe?" Mike demanded. "Christ, is pointing out that he's some regular guy the best you can do? Or worse yet, give everyone your sob story."

"What's wrong with Joe being a person who makes mistakes?"

"He's a god, Petra. We need to make sure people see him that way or there will be no contracts for you to negotiate. No revenue for the agency. No money for your paycheck."

Beyond Mike and his tirade, the radio broadcast played in the background. Petra caught a few words, and then the announcer had her full attention. "In other news, the FBI and other agencies led an early morning raid on a suburban Denver location. The site is rumored to have connections to the new influx of Russian drug trafficking. Now, let's get a look at that rush hour snarl on the interstate…"

Unbidden, Ian came to mind. In truth, he was always at the edge of her thoughts, his name just a whisper in her breath. Had he been at the raid?

The air was thick with disinfectant and stale coffee. A voice continued to buzz in her ear. It was her boss, still talking. What had he said? Something about making Joe take responsibility was distracting to his career and kept people from idolizing him.

Petra pushed open the door to the studio. She inhaled and held her breath for a count of three, then exhaled slowly. The past disappeared. "I disagree," she said, finally joining the conversation. "The days of glorifying celebrities have ended."

"You don't get it," said Mike. "It's the glory that makes them celebrities."

"You heard the interview. Steve Chan wouldn't have accepted my saying that Joe is above the rest of us."

"What I heard was an agent who refused to take control of the interview and get out our message."

"Next time, convince Joe to go on the show. Let him speak for himself if he's done nothing wrong." The sun, a bright white ball, hung in a sky of turquoise blue. Heat shimmered over the expanse of blacktop as she walked across the parking lot. Petra used her remote fob to start her car, a roadster, and unlock the doors.

"And since you mentioned Joe," Mike said, "several sponsors have expressed reservations about renewing his contract. We can't handle another scandal. He's your client. You control him."

Petra's phone beeped. She glanced at the screen. "Speak of the devil," she said. "That's Joe."

"Talk to him, Petra. Get him to clean up his act."

She didn't bother to point out that Mike couldn't have it both ways—either Joe was blameless because he was famous, or he had to behave better. "I'll do what I can."

"You'll get the job done," said Mike, "or find a new one."

Despite the summer's heat, Petra went cold. Sure, her boss was taciturn, but Petra was good at what she did. "Are you threatening to fire me?"

"No. It's a promise."

Mike's call ended abruptly and Joe's immediately came through.

"Petra?" He sounded breathless. "We need to talk."

Was he going to complain about her performance, too? "Hey, Joe, did you hear the interview?"

"No. What interview?"

"I just spent a few minutes with Steve Chan in the Hot Seat."

"Oh, that show can get brutal." He paused a beat. "Listen, something happened. I need you to handle the public relations."

"That's what I was doing, Joe. Public relations, as in talking to Steve Chan about you."

"Well, you might have to visit his show again because this is bigger than big. Lots of heads will roll, you know."

One of those heads, she assumed, would be hers. Her muscles contracted with tension. She rubbed her shoulder with her free hand. "What happened?" she asked.

"I can't talk over the phone. You need to come here, to my house." A beep sounded from Joe's side of the call. "That's my driveway intercom. I'll see you in half an hour." The line went dead.

With the news of the FBI raid still fresh in her mind, she pulled up her friend Katarina Floros's social media page. Katarina worked for Ian as a communications specialist, and two weeks ago she'd posted a picture that Petra hadn't found the courage to "like."

A couple stood before a lake. The Rocky Mountains served as a backdrop, and the water was so clear there were two sets of mountains and two skies. Without question, it was a photo of a couple as they took their vows. The groom, tall and handsome, was someone Petra knew well—Roman DeMarco, another employee of RMJ. The bride was a woman she'd never seen. Katarina's husband officiated the service. Ian Wallace, the best man, stood just behind Roman's shoulder.

It had been two years since Petra ended the relationship with Ian and she had no right to wonder about his life, yet she did. He'd obviously remained in Colorado and hadn't returned to England after their breakup. Had he taken a date to the wedding, and if so, were they serious? She wondered who Roman had married and if Katarina had thrown a bridal shower—it seemed like something Kat would do. Petra glanced at the picture once more, a voyeur into the life she would never live, and shoved the phone into her bag.

As she drove through Denver's more exclusive neighborhoods, Petra's headache returned with a vengeance. She'd been rash to ignore the pain when it first began at the radio station, and now it was a full-blown migraine. Each throb of her pulse exploded like a bomb inside her skull.

The sun beat down, surrounding everything in a brilliant and blinding halo. She gripped the steering wheel with knuckles gone white and rounded the corner. Joe Owens's home came into view.

Made of golden brick, with a set of double doors and a side room that resembled a turret, the three-story home was impressive and immense, even on a street of impressive and immense homes. The wrought iron gate was open—unusual, but then he had told her to come. Since she was expected, Petra didn't bother with the call box. She followed the winding drive to a circular courtyard, where Joe's cobalt blue SUV sat.

Petra parked her car next to his and turned off the engine. She closed her eyes. Inhaled. Exhaled. Again and again. The pain remained, lurking just beneath the surface, like wisps of fog over a river on a sultry night.

After tucking her keys into her handbag, Petra walked to the front door and rang the bell. Far-off chimes announced her arrival.

Nothing.

She gripped the door handle and pulled down. It held fast. She hit the doorbell three times in a row, the chimes playing and replaying, the echo rolling across the courtyard and down the wide lawn.

Her head throbbed with each chime of the bell, and her frustration grew. There was no way Joe hadn't heard her, unless he wasn't home. His car was here, but really, that meant next to nothing. He could have easily been picked up by someone else, or left with the person who'd stopped by earlier, while they'd been on the phone.

Whatever the excuse, her client owed her an explanation. She called his cell phone. It went directly to voice mail.

"Joe." Petra didn't bother to keep the irritation from her voice. "Where the hell are you? I'm here."

She ended the call and rang the bell again. Still no one came to the door.

Petra made a second call to Joe. Again, voice mail

picked up. "Just so you know, your behavior is costing me my job. If I get fired because of you, I'll kill you."

Shoving the phone back into her handbag, she followed the brick walkway to the back of the house. A pool, complete with a slide and whirlpool, was empty. Two tumblers filled with amber liquid and ice sat on a table. Sweat trickled down the side of the glasses. Joe hadn't been gone from his drink for long. But where was he? And who had been drinking with him?

Sunlight glinted off the water's surface. The glare left Petra blind, and the pain in her head was now a thunderous roar. She fumbled in her bag for a set of sunglasses and slipped them on. They did little for the pain, but at least she could see.

Beyond the patio, a set of French doors stood open.

None of what she'd found made sense. Joe valued security even more than privacy. It was unlike him to leave the front gate open and his house seemingly unattended.

Maybe he was home, but doing what? And why ignore Petra, when he had insisted that she stop by? Certainly, visiting a client while sick with a migraine was the worst thing to do. Yet if she could get out of the sun, the worst of her headache might abate.

She approached the threshold and took a tentative step into the family room. Sheer curtains hung from ceiling to floor and billowed in the breeze.

"Knock, knock," she called. "Joe? It's Petra. Are you home?"

From somewhere, she heard a gurgling. Petra

strained to listen. The noise was gone as quickly as it came.

She took another step.

There it was again—a sound like water struggling down a blocked drain.

"Joe?"

Nothing. Not even the sound. With one hand on the wall, she ventured down a darkened hallway. Her heart thudded against her rib cage. With the thunderous pulse, the pain in her head multiplied tenfold. She staggered, almost stumbling, but pushed herself upright and took another step, her fingers trailing along the wall.

Around the edges of her consciousness, she sensed the lurking nothingness that came with a blackout. Then a burst of pain exploded in the back of Petra's skull. She pitched forward, slamming into the tile floor. And then all she knew was darkness.

Chapter 2

Once Ian Wallace decided that Nikolai Mateev had to die, it became easy to bend rules and break laws. He sneaked the computer out of the Comrades' safe house and worked on the laptop in the relative privacy of his black SUV with darkened windows, which was parked two blocks away.

All that ended as he spotted Special Agent Marcus Jones striding purposefully up the street. He wore the obligatory Fed uniform of a dark suit and red tie. In the moment, Ian wondered if the uptight special agent had anything else in his wardrobe.

Ian hit the keys rapidly, then slid the flash drive from the port. He was shutting the laptop's lid as Jones rapped his knuckles on the side window. "What the hell are you doing, Wallace?" the agent asked through the glass. "I'm pretty sure that's my evidence in your hands."

Ian rolled the window down. "This laptop was found—"

"Hidden behind the wall," Jones interrupted. His nostrils flared and the cords in his neck stood out. "I heard. I am with the FBI, you know. My question is why in the hell did you take a laptop from my raid?"

"Technically," said Ian, "I'm the one in charge of the raid."

"I want Mateev as bad as you do, but you're playing with the FBI now and everything—and I mean everything—has to be done by the book," said Jones. "I don't want loopholes that can be exploited during a trial. So just tell me that you didn't try to get into that laptop. If you did, a judge will consider it tainted and we'll never get a search warrant for whatever you found."

Ian's work here was done. He'd hoped to quietly turn the computer in to evidence and leave without seeing Special Agent Jones, much less have a confrontation. Since that wasn't going to happen, Ian only wanted to leave. "I don't want to get into a pissing match with you, but I am the team leader. This computer was found and I wanted to see what was on the hard drive."

Jones paused a beat. "What did you find?"

"Nothing," said Ian. "There's too much encryption to break through."

The FBI agent dragged his hands down his face, giving him a hangdog look. "No offense, but you're the biggest moron I've ever met. That computer is evidence. You know that. Besides, people in this country have rights against illegal search and seizure. They expect that we'll conduct a fair and honest investigation and that a judge will sign warrants before we search their property all along the way."

"Are you done with the lecture on the American legal system?"

"Depends," said Jones. "Did you pay attention?"

"Remember, you hired me to catch Nikolai Mateev because I didn't have to play by all of your rules."

"Consider yourself fired."

Ian shoved the laptop through the open window. "Take your computer. I have everything I need to find Mateev on my own."

"You're off the case. Completely. I don't want to see you or any of your operatives from RMJ anywhere near Mateev. If I do, I'll arrest you all for obstruction of justice. Got that?" Marcus took the offered computer.

Ian didn't answer. He didn't need to. As far as he was concerned, the FBI had served their purpose. Now? Ian didn't need them anymore.

He raised the window and put the SUV into gear, the flash drive safely hidden in his palm. Sure, lying to the FBI and stealing evidence made Ian guilty of more than a dozen federal crimes. But what did he care about a little jail time when it meant sending Nikolai Mateev where he belonged—straight to hell?

* * *

Petra slowly regained consciousness, opening her eyes to find herself leaning against a wall, her hand resting on a gray plastic box. Her head throbbed with each beat.

Beep. Beep. Beep.

The last thing she remembered was a phone call from one of her clients, Joe Owens. He'd wanted to see her, but then what? The beeping grew, climbing in intensity, rising in volume before ending in a crescendo of a full-blown alarm. Petra could almost see the sound waves radiating out from the small gray box. She had tripped an alarm. But why? Nothing made sense.

She took in the rest of the room, which was tiled in cream-colored marble and framed with blond wood. Nearby was a set of double doors, and a staircase on the left led up to a balcony that ran the length of the room.

Like seeing the corner of a photograph, the fragment of a memory came to her. It was Christmastime and she stood in this room—Joe Owens's foyer. She'd spilled red wine on her silk blouse and had been directed to the kitchen where she could get some seltzer water for the stain.

An arched doorway on her right led to the same kitchen. The room beyond was dark. The lights were off and the curtains had been drawn.

Petra caught a glimpse of her dress, her hands. She was covered in splatters of red. Not wine this time. Blood? Icy tendrils of panic reached for her throat and squeezed. Was she bleeding? She scanned her body. Scrapes, bruises, a single cut to her arm. Beyond that, she had the expected residual headache that came after a migraine, and nothing else. So what had happened after she lost consciousness? Why was she covered in blood?

Her handbag lay in the middle of the foyer, the contents were scattered about. Lipstick. Sunglasses. Keys. Wallet. No phone. She dove for her purse and dug into the interior. It was empty.

"Joe?" Her throat was dry, her voice hoarse.

Petra took a step. Her legs trembled, and her vision wavered. She breathed deeply, trying to stay calm. She had to call someone. The kitchen… There'd been a landline in the kitchen. She peered around the corner and found nothing but darkness. Dark floor. Dark walls. Dark forms blending in with the gloom.

"Joe?"

Petra took another step, then another. The floor underfoot was sticky. The odor of copper and meat was thick in the air. The shadow of the island loomed before her. Her foot connected with something solid but not hard. Petra's heartbeat raced.

Scrambling, she reached for the wall. Her hand danced along the surface until she found an electrical switch. She turned it on. The room blazed with light. A pool of black spread out around her feet. Joe lay sprawled at the base of the island with a knife protruding from his side.

Petra sank to her knees next to him. His shirt was soaked and crimson, his breath nothing more than a gasp. She dared not touch the knife, lest she hurt him more.

"Joe? Joe? Can you hear me?" The alarm continued to scream. Petra couldn't even hear her own voice.

He didn't respond.

A loud knocking was heard and above the din a voice called, "Police. Open up."

The police. She scrambled to her feet, lightheaded with gratitude that someone had arrived who could help Joe—help her.

A large man in a suit stood on the stoop. He held up a small leather portfolio. His badge and photo ID were visible. "I'm Detective Sergeant Luis Martinez with the Denver PD. I'm responding to a home alarm." He looked her over from head to toe. "Are you injured, ma'am?"

Petra's legs went weak with relief. She held tight to the doorjamb. "I'm fine," she managed to say, "but you need to help him."

"Help who?" the detective asked.

"He's in the k-kitchen," she stammered, "and hurt."

The detective swept past her as three more black-and-white police cruisers rushed up the drive. Half a dozen officers exited the vehicles and ran to the house.

"That way," she said, pointing to the kitchen as they approached. One of the police officers disabled the alarm. The silence was more terrifying than the noise. In the quiet, Petra could hear a single question echoing in her mind: What have I done?

She leaned on the wall for support. Her throat

burned. She wanted to pass out. But she needed to know what had happened to her client.

She stepped toward the kitchen, but Martinez blocked her path. He had removed his suit coat and splatters of blood stained his wrinkled shirt and tie. Over his shoulder, she saw the uniformed police officers administering first aid to Joe. In the distance, she heard another siren, and through the open front door she caught a glimpse of an ambulance racing up the drive.

"I need to ask you a few questions," Martinez said, steering her to a dining room that was situated on the other side of the foyer. Two EMTs bearing a stretcher entered the house and immediately went to the kitchen, disappearing from Petra's view.

It didn't mean that she couldn't hear what they said. "Starting IV fluids," said a female.

"Starting IV fluids," repeated her partner, a male.

"I see seven stab wounds," said the female.

Seven wounds? She tried to picture herself in a frenzy of what—rage? Fear? In her mind's eye, she saw nothing.

"Ma'am? Are you okay?" the detective sergeant asked. "Can you answer a few questions?"

She nodded.

"Let's start with your name and why you're here."

"I'm Petra Sloane, Joe's agent."

"Can you tell me what happened?"

A thousand images flooded her mind at once. Nothing seemed real. "I have no idea. I can't remember a thing."

"You might be in shock," said the detective. "Take a moment…"

Martinez's words trailed off as the EMTs came from the kitchen. Joe was strapped to the stretcher. His eyes were closed; an oxygen mask covered his mouth and nose. An IV was attached to his arm. Petra watched in silence as they placed her client in the back of the waiting ambulance and sped away.

"I should call someone," she said, as the final scream of the ambulance's siren faded into the quiet morning. "His estranged wife, Larissa, maybe. Or… he has a sister in California." Petra could not recall her name.

"That'll hold for a few minutes," Martinez said. "Let's get back to why you were here. What can you recall?"

Why had she come? Petra closed her eyes and brought back as many details as she could muster. The blinding sunlight. The heat wafting off the pavement. Joe's voice in her ear, quick and clipped, his tone low and almost a whisper.

"Joe called me earlier and asked me to come over right away. He needed to tell me something. I figured there was another scandal."

Martinez removed a notepad and pen from his shirt pocket. He flipped past a few pages before scribbling on a sheet. "Another scandal?" he echoed.

"He'd done some pretty stupid things lately. The stories were all over the press. It's my job to portray Joe in the best light possible in the media. So if he'd had any more missteps, I should be the first to know."

"And did he say what kind of misstep he'd made?"

Petra tried to recall exactly what Joe had said. In reality, he hadn't told her much beyond that he had something important to tell her and heads were going to roll. "I guess he didn't say anything in so many words. Only that something bad had happened."

Martinez wrote in his pad and Petra was forced to wait, grappling with memories that she couldn't quite make clear.

"What time did you arrive?"

Finally, a question she could answer. "About nine thirty."

Martinez looked at a fitness tracker he wore around his wrist. "And what transpired between then and now?"

Petra went cold. She began to tremble. "What?" The word caught in her throat. "What time is it now?"

Martinez pinned her with his dark stare. "Quarter after ten."

The detective thought she had stabbed Joe. She could tell, from the hard set of his jaw and his unwavering gaze. She looked away, because the worst part of it all was that Petra feared he was right.

Ian had gathered his team at an RMJ safe house, a dump of a place in the heart of downtown Denver. The small house had a tiny living room and kitchen on the first floor and two bedrooms upstairs.

He remembered each and every person they'd hidden away in this little house. A presidential candidate after an assassination attempt. A cleric wanted by a terrorist group. Yet he'd never pictured that he'd be here personally, along with his team, in desperate need of a place to lie low.

Was this raid, the one that should've been their crowning glory, really going to be their downfall?

They'd gathered in the kitchen, crammed around the small Formica table—Roman, Cody, Julia and Katarina, along with the rest of the team. The air was filled with the electricity of tension and too many unanswered questions.

Roman was the first to speak. "What the hell happened back there? One minute I'm talking to Comrade Three and the next some FBI agent is telling me to leave the witness alone."

Roman's statement was followed by a chorus of grumbles. Everyone had been just as brusquely routed from the bust.

Ian asked a question of his own. "How many lives do you think Nikolai Mateev has ruined? Nobody knows his name, and yet his actions—his drugs— have affected almost every single person in this city. Have you ever thought about that?"

"What are you getting at, brother?" Roman asked.

Ian shook his head. There was no avoiding the truth. "Jones fired us from the case," he said.

Jaws dropped and eyes widened.

"You're kidding, right?" Roman almost choked on the words.

"There was a computer found at the scene," Ian began. "I took it to my car and tried to hack into the system."

"Aw, hell no," said Roman. "Why would you do a thing like that?"

"I don't have time to wait for subpoenas and warrants and technicians in Quantico to analyze data."

"What did you discover?" This question was asked by Cody.

"That Jones isn't willing to break any rules in order to catch Mateev."

"There are laws, Ian," said Roman. "And if we're breaking laws then we aren't any better than Mateev. It's laws that make us civilized. They make us the good guys."

"I guess that's just it," said Ian. "I can't do this anymore. I can't be one of the good guys if it means that I'll never see justice served."

Julia McCloud was the only female operative at RMJ. From her seat next to Cody, she lifted her hand. "Can you cut the crap, sir? What are you telling us?"

"Aside from the fact that we've been sacked from the biggest case in RMJ history, I'm through. There's no more we can do here. The agency is done." The words burned Ian's throat like acid.

Was he really going to close RMJ? It was almost as bad as when Petra left. Ian knew that then, like now, sacrifices sometimes had to be made.

"Mateev has gotten away too many times. Even if he's caught, he won't go to jail. He's too powerful. He'll slither away somehow like he always has." Ian shook his head and gave a mirthless laugh. "I've become cynical, I guess."

"A cynic?" Roman snorted. "Sounds more like you're a quitter."

Ian's internal temperature spiked. Sweat collected at the nape of his neck, snaking down his back. "I'm not quitting. I just know when I'm beat. I'm—"

"Quitting," Roman interrupted.

Ian wanted nothing more than to set him straight, to share his real plans with his operatives. But to what end? Just so they, too, would be compromised—maybe even criminally so? No. He was their leader. It was his job to protect them. This was the best way he knew how to do that.

"As far as the operatives are concerned, RMJ is closed. Katarina, I'll need you to stay on for the next couple of weeks and help me shut down all the cases."

Roman slapped the table, a sharp crack that rent the air. "I've dedicated my life to this outfit. We all have. Remember when you found me in the hospital, broken both emotionally and physically?"

"What's your point?"

"You promised a world where justice was pursued and light was shone into the darkest corners of the human heart, or some such crap. And now you're quitting?"

"I'm not quitting, brother."

"From where I sit, it looks like you are." Roman shoved his chair back and stood. "And you aren't my brother."

Ian stared at the kitchen table. He slid his hand into his pocket. There, he wrapped his fingers around the flash drive. He hoped that he now held the key that could unlock the last door to Mateev.

If not, Ian had just ruined his life's work for nothing.

The interrogation room was a ten-foot-square space with barely enough room for a faux wood table and two plastic chairs. The walls were covered in cheap paneling and the air stank of stale body odor.

Before leaving Joe's house, Petra volunteered to have her fingerprints taken. Her clothes and purse had been bagged as evidence and she was allowed to wash up. She now wore an extra large white men's T-shirt and large gray sweatpants, along with a pair of flip-flops meant for a giant—all compliments of the Denver PD. She had also been examined by EMTs, who determined that none of her injuries were life-threatening. Then she had been invited to the police station.

The door opened and she looked up. Martinez entered the room, his bulk making the already small space seem even smaller. He squeezed into the second chair and threw a manila file on the table. Even from her seat, Petra could see the indexed title. It was her name.

Her stomach churned. She hadn't been arrested or read her Miranda rights, so she hadn't asked for an attorney of her own. Petra only wanted to be helpful and find out what happened to Joe—no matter the truth. Yet now she couldn't help but wonder if her decision had been prudent.

"Sorry to keep you so long," Martinez said. "Do

you need anything? Water? Coffee? Something to eat?"

She shook her head. "I'm fine."

"I have some more items to discuss that might help clear up what happened with Joe. First, do you recall anything more than what you already told us?"

"There are a few things that I remember, but I don't know how much use they'll be," she said.

He flipped open the file and took out a pen. "Why don't you let me be the judge of what matters and what doesn't."

"It's not a memory exactly, but Joe had several video cameras around his property and even a few in the house…" Petra drew in a breath, fearful of what might have been recorded.

Martinez set his pen aside. "The surveillance system was disconnected. Nothing's been recorded since last night."

That was odd. Still, Petra continued, "The front gate was open. It's controlled by an intercom and Joe always keeps it locked."

"Did you call up to the house when you arrived?"

Petra shook her head. "We had spoken earlier. He said it was urgent and was expecting me, so I didn't bother. That brings up something else. Someone had stopped by when we were on the phone."

"Did he say who?"

Petra shook her head again.

"And then?"

"He didn't answer the front door when I rang the bell." The disorientation she had felt upon waking was gone, although not all her memories had returned. "I even called his cell phone. When that didn't work, I went around by the pool and let myself in through the back. I can't really remember anything after that."

"Your fingerprints were found on the home alarm," said Martinez.

Petra had gotten used to his statements that were really questions. "I think I set it off. The first thing I remember clearly is my hand on the alarm and a lot of beeping."

Martinez nodded and made a note in the file. "How many times did you call Joe?"

"Twice," she said.

"Do you recall throwing your phone into the pool?"

"Is that where it was found?" she asked.

"It was."

"Can I have it back?"

"It's in evidence now. And you haven't answered my question. Do you recall throwing, or dropping, your phone in the pool?"

A blast of cold air shot from a vent in the ceiling. Petra crossed her arms over her chest and tried not to shiver. "I remember walking by the pool." She'd been sick with a migraine and frustrated with Joe. Had she done something stupid, something she didn't remember, then? "I think my phone was in my purse."

"Is that a no?"

"No," Petra snapped. "I didn't put my phone in Joe Owens's pool." She wanted to be helpful, but she had almost reached her limit. "Is this going to take much longer? I did come here voluntarily," she reminded the cop.

"Do you want a lawyer?"

"Do I need one?" she fired back.

"I just have a few more questions, if you don't mind."

Petra blew out a breath. "Sure. Go ahead."

Martinez scribbled a note. "You were on a radio show this morning. Steve Chan's, Hot Seat."

Petra wasn't sure if it was a question or statement. She answered him anyway. "I was."

"And what was the nature of your visit to the show?"

"Joe Owens."

"Anything in particular about Joe?"

Petra didn't like that Martinez kept using her client's first name—as if the championship MVP and the cop were somehow friends. "And how is my client?" she asked.

Martinez shook his head. "Not good."

Petra bit her lip. "Any prognosis?"

Martinez looked at the file, flipping through the first few pages. "None that I know of. Let's get back to the radio interview. Is it true that, on air, you threatened to strangle Joe Owens?"

Her face tingled. Her hands lay on the table, too heavy to lift. Her throat was unbelievably dry. She swallowed. "It was hyperbolic," she said. "You know, for effect."

"I understand hyperbole, Ms. Sloane," said the detective.

She began to sweat. "And besides, Steve Chan made a joke about all of Joe's recent scandals and asked me if I ever wanted to wring his neck."

"And then," Martinez continued, "didn't you threaten to outright kill Joe Owens the second time you called his cell phone?"

"I was angry. I didn't mean anything by it. It was just…"

"Hyperbole," Martinez offered.

"Do I need a lawyer?"

"You tell me. Do you?" He closed the file. "I want to believe that you had nothing to do with the attack on Joe, really I do. But you threatened his life twice today. You were covered in blood when the police arrived, your fingerprints are on the alarm. Yet you claim to have no memories of anything that transpired for over forty-five minutes. What am I supposed to think?"

"I don't know," she said. Her voice was small, even in the tiny room. "I have migraines and sometimes I black out, but can still be on my feet, talking and active. I had an episode this morning."

Lying, or concealing her ailment, would only make things worse, she knew. Why was it that she wanted to keep these most important details from Martinez? Yet Petra wasn't stupid. With her admission she'd certainly become a person of interest—maybe even a suspect.

She dug her fingernails into her palm and continued. "I lost consciousness. That's why I can't remember."

Martinez bounced his pen on the file. Tap-tap. Tap-tap. Tap-tap. "Then I guess I was wrong."

She looked him in the eye. "About what?"

"You do need a lawyer. I'm naming you as a person of interest in the attack on Joe Owens."

For Petra, the next seven hours passed in a haze. She cleared out her savings to pay the retainer for a lawyer who had a reputation for being both honest and brilliant. He'd gotten the police to release her car and her purse, and Petra waited alone by the precinct parking lot. A police officer pulled up next to the curb and said nothing as Petra slid into her seat and drove away.

She felt as if she should call someone and check in. But who? Then again, she didn't have a phone.

With nothing beyond her thoughts for company, she couldn't help but recall the last time she had blacked out. She'd been a sophomore in college and her mother had called to let Petra know that her father's CAT scan looked suspicious. Then Petra found out that her roommate had stolen her boyfriend, when she saw them making out on campus. The headache had begun much like it had today. More than a decade ago, she'd lost almost an hour. When she came to, she'd had a pair of scissors in her hand and had cut her own hair.

What bothered Petra then, as it did now, was the fact that she had the potential to destroy. It was her most closely guarded secret and still she couldn't help but wonder, what did that say about Petra as a person?

She'd never answered the question before. Could she now?

Turning down her street, she saw her condominium complex come into view. The front gate was ablaze with lights from a dozen different TV vans, all the local stations and two cable news networks. Her heart stilled as she stared, wide-eyed. Petra expected that the media would learn of her involvement, but she'd hoped that it would take time, as in days—not hours.

Now what? She eased her foot off the gas and the car slowed.

Petra had no desire to drive through the gauntlet of reporters and questions, to have her privacy invaded by the press. But what else was she supposed to do? Drive around all night?

She heard a sharp knock on her car window. With a start, she turned to the noise. A man in a Colorado Mustangs ball cap stood outside the car. He slapped the glass.

"You," he said, pointing a shaking finger. "I saw you on TV. You deserve to rot in jail until you die for what you did."

In the distance, she saw a group of reporters turn in her direction. Microphones in hand and cameramen on their heels, they ran toward her car. She didn't like her chances in a tussle with the media. Or the crackpot in the ball cap, for that matter.

Jerking the gearshift into Reverse, she dropped her foot on the accelerator. The tires screamed. A cloud of smoke surrounded her. The taste of burning asphalt clung to her lips. She backed up the street, and at the intersection, turned the steering wheel and sped away.

Her heart raced and her pulse thrummed at the nape of her neck. For a time she drove without thought, but all the while Petra knew where she was going. She turned onto the tree-lined street, and her eye was drawn to the Tudor-style home midway up the block. She pulled in to the circular drive and stopped in front of the wooden door. Dark windows stared out like blank eyes. She turned off the ignition and stepped into the rapidly cooling evening air. Petra wrapped her arms over her chest as her flip-flops slapped across the pavement.

She rang the bell. Chimes echoed. The lights remained dark, the house silent.

No one was home, but how long until someone would return? Minutes? Hours? Days?

Coming here was a bad decision, made in a moment of weakness. She considered leaving—renting a hotel room and waiting for the media to get tired of camping out at her condo complex. Then again, she needed more than a place to hide. She needed help and protection. She needed to be here.

Petra made a deal with herself. The door was controlled by an electronic lock. If the combination hadn't been changed, Petra would take it as a sign, and stay. If not, she'd leave.

She pressed the first number. The second. The third. Then she entered the final number. She gripped the handle and pulled down. The door swung open.

She stepped inside and quickly turned on the light.

A grandfather clock stood in the corner and began to ring out the quarter hour. She closed the door and inhaled deeply. The scent was exactly as she remembered, sandalwood and musk and whiskey.

It smelled like him. Ian.

Stepping in farther, Petra ran her hand along the curving newel post. The wood was smooth and warm. Behind her, the door opened. Petra turned at the noise. He stood on the threshold, regarding her with steely gray eyes. He wore black pants and a snug black shirt. His hair was disheveled and stubble covered his cheeks and chin.

Her pulse raced. She gripped the newel post tighter. "Hello," she said.

Ian gazed at her for a moment before kicking the door closed with his heel. "I definitely didn't expect to find you here," he said.

He was neither pleased nor angered. She'd hoped for one or the other, not cool neutrality—especially since energy coursed under her skin, leaving her feeling raw and exposed "I've been accused of attempted murder," she said. "And I need you to help me find out what happened. I want to hire Rocky Mountain Justice."

Chapter 3

Petra's words surrounded Ian like smoke.

The last time they spoke, his job had been the topic. She'd cried. He'd yelled. The accusations had been plentiful on both sides. And now she wanted to hire him? In a day that was anything but smooth, this was the last wrinkle he'd expected.

A bolt of anger shot through Ian. She was the one who'd left—and now she was back, asking for help? Damn her!

He checked his emotions and cleared his throat. "You can't hire me," he said. His stomach clenched into a hard ball of resolve. "I closed Rocky Mountain Justice today."

Petra recoiled as if she'd been slapped. "What do you mean? I thought you were working with the FBI. I heard something on the news this morning that made me think of you…"

"There was a raid," he said, "and we were working together, but we got sacked." Before she could ask why, he added, "I got caught trying to steal evidence."

"I know you, Ian. You're impulsive, but not careless. What's going on?"

He shook his head. He didn't want to talk about it anymore, and even if he did, Ian hardly knew what he would say. Nikolai Mateev was out there and Ian was going to find him. He didn't need this distraction.

"I'm sorry, Petra. I can't help. It's too complicated for me to explain, but without my license, anything I do will be considered illegal. It won't be admissible in court and could send me to jail. And I certainly wouldn't be of much use to you, under the circumstances."

"Sure, I get it," she said. And then added, "I should go." Her gaze traveled from his face to the door. "The media was at my condo, so I'll need to find someplace to stay for the night."

Ian's chest tightened. He knew Petra, knew she'd already be thinking about the next steps in her case. Should she plea-bargain for minimal jail time?

No, Ian couldn't turn her out, not if he could help—even if it was only to hear what she had to say. Maybe he could add some perspective.

"Stay," he said. "Tell me what happened."

"One of my clients was attacked in his home," she said. "The police think I did it."

"And did you?"

"I don't remember."

"Shock?" he asked.

"No. It was a migraine."

Ian had been in business long enough to know that most crimes had as much to do with the victim as the perpetrator. "Which client?" he asked.

"Joe Owens," she said.

"The Mustangs' quarterback?"

"You know him? I thought you didn't really follow American sports," she said, surprised.

"I live in Denver," Ian said pointedly. "The name Joe Owens is hard to avoid."

He paused. Was this all she wanted from him— help? Then again, hadn't he imagined this exact moment time and again where he got a chance to face her, to find out what had led her to walk out on him? She was asking for his help—but looking at her, he was forced to admit all the time she'd called to him from his dreams since she'd left. Although in his fantasies, she had rushed into his arms for solace…and passion.

In the reality of the moment, she remained rooted by the stairs, and the past two years stretched out around him like a desert. It seemed as though little of their once-blazing desire for each other had survived.

Ian studied her face, trying to catalog what had changed since he'd seen her last. There was a scrape on her chin and a bruise to her cheek. But those differences were superficial.

She wore her hair longer than when they'd been together, and even in the baggy clothes, she was still toned with well-defined muscles, he could tell. There were fine lines around her eyes and slight furrows between her brows. Far from the changes making her less attractive, she had gained gravitas and wisdom. In fact, she was more beautiful than before.

Then that begged the question—what changes did she see in him?

"What happened?" he asked, bringing the conversation around to the reason she was in his home.

Petra's fingers trailed along the railing. His gaze followed her touch. Ian's mouth went dry.

"I'm not sure," she said. "Like I said, I don't remember."

Ian wasn't in the mood for a mystery—not tonight. "What do you know?"

Petra spent the next several minutes telling him about the events of the morning. The interview. The call. The migraine. The blackout. Finding the body, the arrest and getting bail. "I couldn't think of any-place else to go," she concluded. "I hope you aren't upset."

For Ian, there were several questions—some more important than the others. He began with one of the most benign. "How about we talk about this over a cup of tea?" He'd never gotten into the coffee habit, despite his colleagues' ribbing about his British tastes.

"Actually," she said with a sigh, "that'd be nice."

The kitchen was beyond the foyer, and for the first time, Ian saw it as a sterile place—one without use or meaning. The granite countertops and cherry cabinets were wiped clean and sparkled as if in a commercial for lemon-scented cleanser.

It was completely opposite from when he'd lived with Petra. When she was here, the aroma of coffee always filled the house. The island in the center of the kitchen was covered with dishes, a smudge or two on the appliances. At the time, he'd found it too chaotic. And now? He missed the disorder, the sense of home she'd brought to his life.

Who was he kidding? She'd been his home—and he'd been too focused, too obsessed with his target to appreciate everything he had with her.

He set the pot to boil. "You're in a mess," he said. "But why come to me? This isn't exactly the type of case that RMJ handles."

"Like you said. I am in a mess and isn't that your specialty? People with problems?"

It wasn't the answer he was looking for. Ian needed to hear Petra say that she needed him. Yet she hadn't.

She sighed, "I'm not trying to escape the consequences, even if it means some time in jail."

Ian tried to admire her bravery, her character. Still, this was Petra, the woman he loved. Had once loved, he corrected, if only to himself.

"Some time in jail?" he echoed her sentiment, each word dripping in incredulity. "You can end up spending your life behind bars. Or worse. Colorado is a death penalty state, you know."

Her eyes glistened with unshed tears. It was the first sign of vulnerability and it cut Ian to the core.

"I'm scared," she said. "Scared I did something

horrible. Scared that I'll be prosecuted for something I didn't do—or worse, that I did but can't remember doing. Scared that I'll never know the truth."

Her words trailed off. Ian wanted nothing more than to wrap her in his arms, to keep her fears at bay. Yet he couldn't—shouldn't—touch her.

He asked instead, "Why did you come to me, Petra?"

"I want to know what happened," she said. "No matter what, you can find the truth."

The kettle began to boil. At least he could offer her the comfort of a cup of tea. He filled a cup with water and a tea bag before handing it to Petra. "Sugar," he said. "No cream."

She looked down and smiled, as if to herself. "You remembered."

How could he not? Everything about Petra was unforgettable.

Petra scooped in sugar and stirred her tea. The silver spoon hit the side of the china cup, filling the room with a tinny chime. "I guess what really bothers me is that I feel like a ticking time bomb. I'm worried that I'm actually dangerous to everyone—my clients, my friends, my family."

Ian reached for her wrist, stilling her hand. "I'll be honest, I have a hard time picturing you being violent—even if your job was at stake and you were frustrated."

Petra kept her eyes on the counter. "I'm not so sure I agree with you."

"Here's the way I see it. Joe Owens is a big bloke— you're easily half his size. He's strong and not likely to let you stab him without a fight. Where are your wounds? Why aren't you bruised from head to toe?"

"But what if I surprised him?"

"What? While stumbling through his house, blind with a migraine? It's not in your nature to attack someone for no reason."

"I had a reason," she insisted. "My boss threatened to fire me because of Joe."

"Granted, you're driven—but a life for a job? It hardly seems like an equal trade."

She pressed her lips together. "I wasn't exactly in control. There's no telling what I might have done and no way to gauge my actual strength in that fugue state."

A tremor ran down his spine. Petra's honest nature might well be her undoing.

"You didn't point any of this out to the police, did you?" Ian continued with a warning, "Remember those Miranda rights. Anything you say is likely to be used against you."

"Are you telling me to lie?" she asked.

"I'm telling you not to make it too easy."

"Understood," she said with a nod.

Petra's situation was like a puzzle box, with only one way to solve it, and thousands of ways to be wrong. His mind began to work and he lighted on a rather simple fact. "You never saw or spoke to Joe after you arrived, correct? He could've been attacked and then left for dead."

"But if I didn't attack Joe, who did?" she asked.

"Who else might want him dead?"

She shook her head. "I can't think of anyone. Everyone loved Joe Owens. He was a hometown hero. Championship MVP."

"Obviously, someone didn't."

Petra took a sip of her tea. A bead of tea collected on her lip. She licked it away.

God help him, an image of his lips on hers, his mouth claiming her, their tongues intertwined, came to Ian and left him wanting more than a memory.

He picked up his own tea and gulped down a swallow. The liquid scalded him. Then again, he'd been burned by her before. Passion and pain were opposite sides of the same coin, and in that regard, with Petra, he'd been a wealthy man.

"You said you were on the radio talking about Joe and his most recent scandal…" He let his words trail off so that Petra could fill in the facts.

"He threw a punch at a reporter for asking an embarrassing question at yesterday's press conference. Last week he yelled at a waitress and his tirade ended up on the internet. Then the week before, he was arrested for disturbing the peace at a nightclub."

"Was the reporter seriously hurt? Any reason to want vengeance?"

Petra shook her head. "Joe only got in a punch or two before being dragged out of the room. The incident made the reporter famous. He was contacted by a cable sports channel and called our agency for representation. The waitress was given twenty-thousand dollars by the team and she enrolled in college. No one wants to get even."

"And the police wouldn't try to kill someone who got rowdy at a club."

"Doubtful," Petra agreed.

"There has to be something else. Nobody is completely beloved. What about his personal life?"

"Joe's wife moved out of their house at the beginning of the summer and took their daughters with her," she said, leaning back in her seat, her hands wrapped around the cup of tea. "There were rumors that she was having an affair, but he was fighting any divorce proceedings."

"She wouldn't be the first woman to want an estranged husband dead so she could be with her lover."

"It's more than that," said Petra. "Joe's wife, Larissa, was supposedly seeing Arnie Hatch, the team's owner."

"Is there any truth to the stories?"

Petra nodded absently. "It's one of the worst kept secrets in Denver's sports scene."

"Then I say we have two suspects—Arnie Hatch and Larissa Owens."

"We? Does that mean I can hire you?"

"Like I said—RMJ is closed."

What Ian said was true, but that was only in a technical sense. He was still in business, still able to take cases. And while he wanted to help Petra, he needed to find Mateev. Making the mistake of listening to his conscience, he added, "It doesn't mean I can't look into the case a little bit tonight. If I find anything interesting, I'll let you know. You can turn it over to your lawyer."

Petra gave a long exhalation, slumping in her seat. "You don't know how relieved I am. So, what do we do now?" she asked.

"You are going to finish your tea and then you can sleep in the guest room. I'll do some research on Hatch."

Petra took another drink and pushed her cup to the center of the island. "Thanks for everything, Ian. You're a lifesaver and I don't know what I'd do without you."

He picked up both cups and turned to the sink. He ran water from the tap, scrubbing away the residue. Glancing at the window, he watched Petra in the reflection. "There are some of your things in the dresser upstairs." She looked up, meeting his gaze. He dropped his eyes to the faucet and turned off the water. "You left them and I never got around to returning them or putting them out with the rubbish."

"Lucky me."

"Always a little sarcastic. I still don't know what to make of you."

She rounded the island and stood behind him, her breath warming his back. He turned. Petra was close—so close that he could touch her if he just reached out. And if he did, what would she do?

"I truly am lucky," she said. Her voice was sultry, like a night too hot and humid for sleep. "Because you're right. I am in a mess, and before I showed up here, I worried that I was guilty. And now there's some hope that I'm not."

"You're welcome, then," he said, before adding, "I

know our relationship didn't end well, but I'm glad you came to me. I'm happy to help, even if it's just a little."

He reached out, his hand grazing her wrist. She stiffened but didn't pull away. Ian took that as a good sign and let his fingers trail up her arm. His hands remembered the feel of her flesh. His lips remembered her kisses. His body remembered what it was like to be with hers.

Then again, did he want to get involved with Petra? Hadn't they had their shot at happiness and wholly missed the mark? Beyond the breakup, there was the aftermath. Two years and nothing—not even a damn email. Could he relive those dark days after she'd left, when Scotch was his only friend?

No, Ian could not—would not—let himself stumble off that cliff a second time.

And yet his fingers burned with the need to touch her.

He bent his head, his mouth brushing her cheek. She exhaled, a quiver in her breath. It was all the encouragement he needed. His lips found hers and he wrapped his arms around her waist, drawing her to him. For Ian, Petra was the best bad choice he could ever make.

Petra pressed her body into Ian's. His strong arms wrapped around her waist, pulling her closer to him. He was an intoxicating mix of commanding and dangerous; and tonight, Petra intended to get drunk on her former lover.

She parted her lips and his tongue slipped inside her mouth. Too soon, too fast, she was consumed by the kiss.

Ian gripped her neck and pulled back, exposing her throat as he covered her with kisses. With his other hand, he cupped her breast. His touch was light and her nipple hardened at once. He deepened the kiss, claiming her, making Petra a captive of her own unchecked lust.

Head bent, he kissed her breast, wetting the cotton fabric, his tongue dancing over her nipple. She moaned with ecstasy that she could no longer contain. How long had it been since someone had had this effect on her? How long had it been since her desires had been so ignited?

The questions weren't hard to answer. It was when she'd last been with Ian. He was something she'd promised never to do again, and yet—here she was.

When his hand skimmed her waistband, Petra quit thinking. Flesh on flesh, his fingers moved lower and lower. He touched the silky fabric of her panties. She was wet, and her innermost muscles clenched with longing and desire. Even though in the back of her mind, she knew this was the worst kind of mistake.

He rubbed the top of her sex, filling her with molten gold, and she no longer cared.

"Ian," she moaned. "Oh, Ian, I've missed you—I've missed us."

He broke away from the kiss and lifted her onto the island before situating himself between her parted thighs. He was already hard. She arched her back, pressing herself into him. Even with the layers of clothes separating them, the feeling was delicious.

"Do you want me?" he asked, his voice husky. "Tell me you want me."

It would be so easy to love Ian again, especially since she'd never really stopped caring. Then again, what was love if they didn't want the same life? She already knew the answer—it was an empty sentiment that led to heartache and loneliness.

She placed her hands on his chest and pushed firmly. Sliding from the island to the floor, she pressed the back of her hand to her mouth, not trapping the kiss, not wiping it away. Her fingers trembled. "I shouldn't have come here. I'm sorry. I should leave."

"And go where? You said yourself that the media has camped out at your apartment. Don't be daft," he said, his voice without a shred of emotion. "Stay."

Petra gritted her teeth at his calm. She was nothing more than feelings and second-guesses. "Do you always have a stiff upper lip?"

"I suppose so. It goes with the tea and the affinity for British cars."

"And your dry sense of humor."

"There's that, too. By the way, I was wondering— how did you get in?"

The kiss and the passion and the dreams of the future—or rather, the past—were gone for Ian. She needed to drive them all from her mind and her heart, too. "You hadn't changed the code for the lock," she said. "I supposed that since I could still get in, you might be willing to help me…"

Ian shrugged. "I guess I never thought that you'd come back."

It wasn't the answer she wanted. She wanted Ian to confess that he'd kept the same code deliberately, all the while hoping for her return. Sure, he wanted her, even now—the kiss had proved that. But sex and passion had never been their problem. It was the emotional connection she craved, the knowing that he would be there if she needed him. "I couldn't think of anyone else to ask for help. Will you," she asked, "still help me? Even after…" She paused, not sure how to characterize what had just happened. "Even after everything?"

"Like I said, I'll do some digging tonight and see what turns up. From there, you go to your attorney. Agreed?"

She paused again. This time it was for another indelicate subject—money. After all, he was a professional and well paid for his services. She knew; she used to live with him.

Sure, Petra had her own job. But while she was far from poor, she'd emptied her savings account to retain her attorney. She swallowed. "How much will it cost?"

Ian waved her question away. "Don't even mention that to me. Now go upstairs and try to get some rest."

Rest? She could hardly imagine sitting down, much less sleeping. "You said you have some of my clothes?"

Ian raked his hair back. "In the dresser, upstairs guest room."

Oh yes, he had told her that already. "Then I guess I better…" Her throat burned and tightened, her words trailing off.

"I'll let you know what I've found out about Arnie Hatch's background in the morning."

To Petra, it seemed as if the events that led her here had happened years ago and not mere hours. Yet there had been a brief instant while Ian held her that transcended time. In those short moments, Petra had truly felt safe, as if nothing could hurt her.

Ian was now at the sink, rinsing out the teacups. She regarded his form, his broad shoulders and narrow waist—and that rock-hard butt. Without question, he was gorgeous.

But it was what Petra knew about him that made Ian more than appealing. His hair wasn't just blond, with golden and copper strands woven throughout. His eyes, a stormy gray, actually began as silver near his iris and darkened to charcoal at the edge of his pupil. He had a dimple on his lower back that she had kissed countless times and a scar atop his foot.

Even more important than his looks were his character and unwavering confidence, his dedication and strength. Ian was the kind of man women wanted and men wanted to be.

"Can I help with Arnie? I've met him before and—"

Ian didn't turn around. "I work better alone."

Alone.

There it was again. She should have known better than to offer. "Thank you, then," she said, "for everything."

"You're welcome."

Petra waited a moment for him to glance her way. She wanted to look him in the eyes so he'd know... what? Well, that was a question she couldn't answer.

Without another word, she left the kitchen. The guest room was just as it had been when she'd lived in the house. Thick tan carpet covered the floor. One wall was navy blue and the rest painted an unblemished white. There was a matching navy-and-white comforter on the bed, along with a dresser, a TV on a stand and a bedside table with a lamp. In fact, it was almost as if it hadn't been used since she left.

She opened the top drawer of the dresser and found half a dozen pairs of her underwear and a few bras, neatly folded. The next drawer held several shirts, two pairs of jeans and a sundress. In the closet, she found an old pair of her ballet flats.

When she'd walked out, she'd forgotten that she'd been doing laundry, until she went to put on her favorite shoes and couldn't find them. And Ian? He'd never called, either. Never wrote, never texted. In fact, she'd wondered many times if he'd found her clothes—even though they were left in the dryer and hardly something he'd miss.

Petra shut the closet door and went to the adjoining bathroom. She flipped on the light. A face stared at her. She looked over her shoulder, a ready scream on her lips, but found no one there. She looked back and, sadly, recognized the reflection was hers—but not.

Her hair was a tangled mess; her eyes were lost to the dark circles that surrounded them. Her skin was pale and washed-out. Droplets of red lined her cheek—blood? Basically, she looked as feral as she felt.

She turned on the shower, as hot as the tap allowed. Steam rolling out the open glass door collected on the mirror, finally obscuring her image. After stripping off the bulky sweatpants and T-shirt, Petra wondered if burning the outfit would be overly dramatic. With a wry smile, she decided that, yes, it would be a bit much, and she stepped into the spray.

The water was scalding, turning her skin bright red. She jumped back with a yelp, before easing under the shower. The heat didn't bother Petra then. It was minor compared to the burn she still felt for Ian. She grabbed a bar of soap and worked it into a lather, sliding her foamy hands over her body. Why had she pulled away from him when he'd offered what she wanted? Wouldn't the comfort she found in his arms be the best salve for her wounded soul?

Chapter 4

Petra, showered and in fresh clothes, sat on the edge of the bed. She was beyond exhausted, yet questions dogged her. How had the media found her home? What was being reported about the incident at Joe's? Finally, what was the news saying about her?

She grabbed the remote and pushed the power button. The evening newscast filled the screen. Two camera-ready anchors, one male and the other female, sat behind a desk. As the intro music faded, they turned toward the camera.

"Tonight is a sad night in Denver," said the woman. "Joe Owens, quarterback for the Colorado Mustangs, is in critical condition and fighting for his life."

"That's right, Sue," said the man. "It was a vicious attack on the championship MVP that put him in the hospital. At ten fifteen this morning, an alarm was tripped in the Belcaro residence of Joe Owens. Police arrived on the scene within minutes to find that Owens had been stabbed seven times and had lost a tremendous amount of blood."

A picture of Petra, taken from her work's website, flashed on the screen as the anchors spoke. Petra felt ill.

"The police found Joe Owens's agent, Petra Sloane, at the residence and covered in blood. According to police reports, Sloane was unable to recall what transpired for forty-five minutes."

"I bet she can't," said the man, with a sneer.

"We have to wonder what would cause someone, like Sloane, to attack her client. We have with us in the studio psychologist Doctor Douglas Warner."

The camera cut to Dr. Warner, a balding man with a goatee.

"Doctor, can you tell us what might drive a person to commit such a heinous act?"

Dr. Warner said, "Acts, such as this one, are filled with rage. For Ms. Sloane, I think this attack was very personal. I'm certain that Ms. Sloane has other acts of violence in her past. Moreover, I'm also sure that there was a trigger for this event."

Sue, the anchor, looked back at the camera. "Thank you, Doctor Warner. We tried to reach Ms. Sloane for comment. She has not been seen since her release from police custody. Her employer has also been contacted, and they have no comment. Up next, we'll take a look at the career of a football legend, Joe Owens."

It was worse than being naked; she had been completely exposed and examined. Petra turned off the TV and began to pace, as if she could put distance between herself and what had been said on the news. Yet she knew better. Once allegations like the ones leveled at her were made public, they stayed with a person forever. Like she'd been branded by what the reporters said, Petra would always carry the scar of the police accusations.

Yuri Kuzntov had spent an entire day on the run. So far—he hadn't been caught by the cops who were certainly looking for him. It was well past midnight on a day that began with his safe house being raided and he needed to hide for the night.

He broke the column around the steering wheel, revealing a tangle of filaments and plastic. He glanced out the window before pulling two wires free and touching their exposed ends together. The engine started. Yuri slid the gearshift into Drive and pulled onto the street.

It was luck that they'd all risen before dawn and not been caught in their beds. Luck that he'd been in the kitchen when the door was knocked in. It was even luckier that he'd thought to grab a knife and had managed to overpower the cop in the yard. But if his luck held, he'd be able to get a new identity, the necessary paperwork and enough money to leave the country.

There was only one place to get that kind of assistance. Quickly making a U-turn, he drove through the quiet neighborhoods, heading for the address he'd committed to memory weeks ago.

The traffic light turned green and Yuri rolled across the intersection. Confident he hadn't been followed or seen, he pulled in to a pharmacy parking lot and left the car in a space at the rear of the building. Within a minute, he was off the street and in the courtyard of a three-story apartment complex. Head down, he climbed the stairs and knocked on a door.

The door remained closed; the apartment beyond was silent.

He knocked again.

Finally, an answer came. *"Da?" Yes?*

"Eto ya, Yuri." *It's me, Yuri.*

The door opened. A large man with a dark crew cut stood on the threshold. Yuri recognized him as a former FSB officer. Anatoly Shubin now worked as a bodyguard and driver for some of the richest and most ruthless men in Russia.

"What do you want?" he asked.

"The house was raided."

Anatoly opened the door further. "Get inside."

It was a studio apartment—living area, kitchen to the side, an unmade bed and a folding table. It had been decorated in early American ugly—the sofa was upholstered in brown floral fabric and there were two easy chairs in coordinating tweed. The small makeshift dining table was covered in prescription bottles and Chinese takeout containers.

The stench of rot hung in the air, like a sulfurous fog. Three men filled the already cramped room.

Aside from Anatoly, there was another FSB agent, Ilya—also a bodyguard. Then there was the third man, the one in charge.

Nikolai Mateev.

His skin was the color of old paste, his face little more than a skull covered with withered skin. He sat on the sofa, a shriveled and diminished man.

Yuri was having second thoughts. Maybe coming here for help had not been the wisest choice.

Nikolai asked, "What happened?" Despite his shrunken appearance, his voice was strong and commanding, his stare still piercing and keen.

"The police came at dawn," Yuri said. "They raided the house. I stabbed one and ran over another—he might be dead."

Ilya cursed under his breath. "Every cop in Colorado must be looking for you."

"You brought the laptop with you?" Nikolai asked.

"No, *otets*, I did not." *Otets. Sire. Father.*

"Where is it?"

The laptop. It held all Nikolai Mateev's personal and professional information. The otets had brought it with him from Russia and given it to Yuri for safekeeping. He'd hidden it behind the wall of an upstairs bedroom. It might stay hidden forever, but if not the encryption would take weeks to process. Yet that answer wouldn't be acceptable, not to Nikolai, at least.

"It was destroyed," Yuri lied. "Last week."

"What did you do with the computer afterward?" Ilya asked. Like Anatoly, he was large and pale. The only difference was that Ilya had light hair, where Anatoly's was dark.

"After?" Yuri echoed.

"After you destroyed the computer, what did you do with it? If you left it in the safe house the FBI will have pieced it back together by now."

Yuri wiped a hand across his sweaty neck. "I threw it away—out of town, past the airport about two miles. There's a road and I just threw it out the window."

"I know where that is," said Ilya. "You took me there once. It's where you picked up the shipment of heroin."

"Yeah," said Yuri. Let him think what he wants. "That's the place."

"What if you led the *police* here?" Anatoly asked.

"I'm resourceful. I made sure I wasn't followed."

Ilya asked, "If you're so resourceful, then why did you come here?"

"I need a passport, and money." Sweat dampened Yuri's back and his shirt clung to his skin. He'd have to do more than leave Colorado. After this, he'd have to disappear. Maybe go somewhere in South America— Argentina, perhaps.

"You're sure about the computer. You destroyed it…" said Nikolai.

"I smashed it to bits with a hammer and then drove the debris out past the airport."

"That wasn't your job," said Anatoly. "What if you were seen on the road, maybe by a state trooper? There could be an alert out for you."

Nikolai waved away the FSB agents' concerns. "Unfortunate things happen, and this will all end well. You know what to do."

Yuri exhaled. He'd held on to his luck, after all.

"Thank you…" he began.

From behind, strong fingers gripped his throat, making it impossible to speak—or even breathe. Yuri clawed at the hands, but the grip tightened. Tighter. Tighter. His lungs burned. He pitched backward, slamming both him and Anatoly into a wall.

His throat collapsed. Blood pounded in his ears. As death came to claim him, he heard one last voice.

The words were muffled and indistinct. With the last bit of life, he strained to make out what was being said.

"Call him," Nikolai said.

Him who? Yuri tried to speak, but fingers were clamped hard on his throat, choking off his words—his life.

"What do you want me to do with Yuri?"

Nikolai replied, "Dump his body out past the airport and find that damn computer."

And then Yuri's luck ran out.

Always on the lookout for cops, Anatoly kept his eyes on the rearview mirror as he drove. It wouldn't do to get pulled over, since his identity papers were false. But more than that, the police wouldn't look kindly at the corpse Anatoly had stowed in the trunk.

Streetlights hung over the interstate, turning the world an artificial orange. It burned into his corneas and filled his vision with dancing dots. He would've preferred the dark.

"That's it," said Ilya, who sat in the passenger seat. "Take that exit there."

Anatoly pulled on the steering wheel and the large sedan veered off the highway. A sickening thud came from the trunk as Yuri's body shifted with the movement.

"Are you sure you know where you're going?" Anatoly asked.

"Yuri took me here once, before he had to stay in that house and guard the computer. Said he meets street dealers way out here. Nobody ever bothers him."

"Why would he dump something as important as Nikolai's computer in a place where dealers rendezvous?"

"What would they care about some more garbage?" Ilya asked. "To them, it's nothing."

"But why all the way out here?"

His fellow Russian was silent for a moment. "Because he knows the place."

It had been a guess at best, Anatoly knew. At worst, because of Ilya, they were on a fool's errand. When they returned empty-handed they would have to deal with Nikolai's wrath.

Anatoly didn't want to be the next corpse in a trunk.

"Turn there," Ilya said. "On the left."

The headlights illuminated a dusty track that seemed to disappear into the night. He followed the road through the darkness. At one point, Anatoly had been a well-respected FSB officer. He had status. Women. Not a lot of money, though, and that had been his downfall. Greed.

The lust for more rubles had put him in the service of a deranged old goat who sent him out in the middle of the night looking for something that was impossible to find.

Not for the first time, Anatoly wondered why he didn't quit. He had money now.

But he knew the answer. Nikolai Mateev was not a man you loved, but feared.

"Up here," he said. "Right after the rise."

The car crested the hill. The body rolled in the trunk, a hollow thump, like a melon being dropped on a hot street.

"Here," said Ilya.

After sliding the gearshift into Park, he unlocked the trunk with the push of a button. "I'll get rid of Yuri. You find the computer."

Anatoly didn't wait for Ilya's response. He stepped into the night and exhaled, his breath appearing as a frozen mist. Only August, he thought, and already the nights were cold. He opened the trunk and a light came on.

Anatoly hadn't felt sadness in years, and he didn't feel a shred of remorse for having killed Yuri. After all, it was his job. And still Anatoly couldn't help but think that Yuri had been unwise to believe that Nikolai Mateev might help.

Looping his arms under the cold shoulders, Anatoly dragged the body out of the car, then to the side of the road.

He met Ilya as they both came out of the dark, heading for the car. Ilya's breath caught in a cloud of frost. "It's not here."

Anatoly wasn't surprised, and yet a chill that had nothing to do with the temperature crept up his spine. He glanced around at the miles of nothingness; they could almost be on the moon.

He knew how Yuri worked. It was the same with drug dealers everywhere. He'd picked an out-of-the-way spot to meet distributors, where goods were traded for cash, and there were no street cameras to accidentally record the transaction.

"Are you sure?"

"Positive. What do we tell Nikolai?" At least Ilya was smart enough to be scared. "What if Yuri left the laptop at the house? What if the *police* found it?"

"And if that's the case," said Anatoly, "we are as good as dead."

Ian sat in his home office, next door to the guest room where Petra was staying. The screen on his desktop computer cast the only light in the darkened room. He stared at the monitor yet saw nothing beyond color. The shower in the guest suite had stopped running hours ago, and he imagined that Petra had gone to bed. Alone. Without him.

What would she do if he went to her room? If he kissed her again, stroked her hair, her skin, pulled the sheet from her body...

Damn it. Since when did he push himself on women seeking his protection? Even if that woman was his ex—and there was definitely unfinished business between them?

No. It was best to view Petra only in a professional manner, their past notwithstanding.

He turned his thoughts from all things Petra Sloane and focused on the computer. He opened a remote program, one that was running on the RMJ's secure server. It was trying to access the information from the flash drive. Lines and lines of code—all ones and zeros—marched across the screen. He snorted. Even his powerful program had failed to break the encryption. Then again, the Russians were among the top tech experts in the world, and Ian knew enough to be patient.

He then opened the Denver Mustangs website and brought up a picture of the team's owner, Arnie Hatch.

A stocky and balding man in his late fifties, Hatch wore slacks and an oxford shirt with a blue-and-orange tie. The shirt collar was too tight, and Arnie's thick neck sagged over the fabric. He sat on the edge of a practical wooden desk. Stacks of files and papers towered around him. At his back, a wall of windows overlooked the playing field. Much like a busy but humble ruler, Hatch kept a watchful eye on his kingdom.

Ian had never met Arnie Hatch in person, but that didn't mean he knew nothing about the man. More even than his players, Arnie was the most famous man in Denver.

Born to a teenaged mother in Chicago, Arnie had moved to Colorado after buying a small interest in a company that refined shale into natural gas. In the mid-1970s an oil embargo hit and the price of shale oil went sky-high. Arnie sold his interests, making himself rich. Then the industry went bust and he purchased back the company for a fraction of its original value. After that, his company began mining uranium.

Now he was the richest man in the state.

A more advanced search turned up an email account for Hatch. Ian opened up all the messages. With his clearance, it wasn't necessarily illegal. And in truth, where Petra was concerned, Ian wasn't worried about niceties or legalities. Besides, he'd offered to help her for one night and he'd do everything in his power to prove her innocence.

He scanned the subject list. Joe Owens's name appeared more than once. In an email thread with the Denver team's coach, Ian learned that Joe's problems dated back to last season. Hatch had ordered several drug tests, all of which came up clean, and both owner and coach were at a loss for the change in Joe's conduct.

There were also romantic emails between Hatch and Joe's estranged wife, Larissa. The two had traveled to Europe over the summer, which was a badly kept secret, and Larissa now lived in an upscale penthouse paid for by Hatch.

In short, Joe Owens was a problem for the wealthy

businessman. But there was nothing damning—nothing to connect Hatch to the attack.

What if Petra was right? What if everyone in Denver did love Joe Owens? What did that mean for her? Ian sat back, pinching the bridge of his nose. There had to be something…

He reread the list of emails, a long, blurry line. Then he noticed something and looked back. A message dated two days prior was from Hatch to the owner of the Kansas City Cyclones, Kyle Berg. The subject line read Confidential Trade.

Ian opened the first message.

From ArnieHatch@CMfootball.com
To Bergk@KCCyclones.net
8/19
2:43 PM MST
Kyle,
I'd like to set up a call to discuss the upcoming season's roster. I'm interested in Roberts, the tight end. You can have Joe Owens in return.
Arnie

From Bergk@KCCyclones.net
To ArnieHatch@CMfootball.com
8/19
6:56 PM CST
What's the catch? Joe Owens was last year's championship MVP. Why let him go?
Berg

From: ArnieHatch@CMfootball.com
To: Bergk@KCCyclones.net
8/19
5:57 PM MST
Kyle,
To be honest, there's a QB I want from the Canadian Football League who will work better with our running game but signing him sends me over the salary cap. Taking Joe off my books would free up a lot of money. Cutting him is a breach of contract and I'd be out the money anyway. I can trade him until the end of this week. It's a great deal for you.
Arnie

From: Bergk@KCCyclones.net
To: ArnieHatch@CMfootball.com
8/20
9:00 AM CST
I've done some research and have to say that Joe has too many problems off the field. He's a good player but an extreme liability. I'm going to have to pass on the trade. Thanks anyway.

Hatch had then forwarded the entire thread to the coach, including a curt three-line message.

I have to do something about Joe. The drug tests we arranged haven't turned up anything. Stay tuned for updates.

That message was sent on August 20 at 2:00 p.m.,

less than twenty hours before Joe Owens was attacked. There was probably enough evidence for Ian to go to the police with what he had found.

Then again, Hatch would lawyer up. Once the lawyers discovered that Ian had hacked into the system, none of the emails would ever be considered in the case, making the prosecution of Hatch nearly impossible. No, Ian didn't want Petra tangled up in a legal web that he personally helped to weave.

At the same time, Ian could smell the guilt coming off Hatch, like a rotting fish at the edge of the water. There had to be more and he owed it to Petra to find out what it was.

He shut down Arnie's email and pulled up Joe Owens's cell phone records from the carrier's site. He quickly scanned the contact list, looking for anything that caught his eye.

The final entry. Y.K.

Ian's vision cleared, his brain no longer fatigued. Y.K. Yuri Kuzntov—Comrade One. Or maybe Ian was confused. Because what were the chances that the most popular player in the league could be mixed up with a Russian national wanted by the FBI?

He opened up the contact and searched for texts. Within minutes, Ian was looking at an exchange from ten days prior.

Joe: Can you hook me up?

Y.K.: No

Joe: Srsly?

Y.K.: On house arrest

Ian's heart skipped a beat. House arrest? As in not leaving a house—like the three Comrades? He read on:

Joe: I just need a little. I can come to you.

Y.K.: Can't help you out

Joe: You're the only one, man. My special juice is making me crazy. W/o you ima wreck.

Well, that clinched it. Y.K. was obviously providing Joe with drugs. Yuri Kuzntov was a drug dealer. There were too many coincidences for this to be chance.

Using the contact number for Y.K., Ian found the phone. It came up as a pulsating green dot on a map filled with blue highways, green pixelated forests and yellow plains. And yet the location couldn't be right.

He compressed the image again and again.

The phone had been left in the middle of nowhere—two miles east of the Denver airport. And if the time stamp was accurate, which Ian believed it to be, the phone had been stationary for more than an hour.

It could be that Yuri had dropped his phone. But what would a Denver drug dealer be doing miles away from anything in the first place? Yet Ian knew what he was likely to find. It wasn't a person, or a missing phone, but a body.

And if Ian did find a dead Russian—one with ties to Nikolai Mateev? It could be Ian's way back in to the case and eventually to Mateev. Then again, if he was right, Petra was in more danger than either one of them might have guessed.

Chapter 5

Petra lay in the dark, staring at the ceiling. The sounds and smells of the house were soothing and familiar—bringing her back to a time when she had dared to hope for love, not to merely work. At the same time, Joe was everywhere. His bloodied body was the shadowy form in the corner. His face was the reflection off the TV screen. His labored breathing was her own shallow breath.

She wondered if she really had attacked her client. Maybe they had argued, and if so, about what? She tried to imagine the feel of the knife in her hands. Her fingers gripping the wooden handle as the cold steel blade did its cruel work. Had she really wielded it?

Or was Ian right: did she lack the fortitude to kill?

And even if she wasn't involved, if she couldn't

remember what had happened, how would she ever prove her innocence?

Which brought her back to the original question: if not Petra, then who had attacked Joe Owens?

She heard a sound, just a whisper of movement outside her door. Petra's breath froze in her chest. "Ian?" she murmured to the night.

The door slowly opened. He materialized from the darkness, a shadow made whole. "Ian?" she said again. "Is that you?"

"I'm sorry," he said. "I was just doing some work next door. Hope I didn't wake you."

"I wasn't asleep. I just heard you walk by." She toyed with the idea of leaving well enough alone. Then, without much thought, she continued. "There was so much blood. It was everywhere." She lifted her palms and stared at them, despite the dark. "I can still feel the blood on my hands."

"It's tough to see what you saw, to go through what you did," he said. "It may be a while before you can sleep well."

"Might be," she said, if only because the silence was too much to bear.

In the quiet, she could hear her own thoughts—questioning her guilt, taunting her weaknesses. "Late to be working."

"You know me. Once I find something important, I can't let it go. Like a dog with a bone, I suppose."

But not her. He had let Petra slip through his fingers without a second thought. Then again, now wasn't the time to be petty. "What'd you find?"

"I'm not sure. It could be something—or nothing. Either way, I won't know until I check it out."

Petra's heart began to pound against her chest. "Now? In the middle of the night?"

"I don't want it gone by the morning."

"It?"

"Listen, it's almost one o'clock. I should get going so I can get back."

Before she even thought about what she was doing, Petra was on her feet. "No way. I'm going with you. I can't stay alone, not now."

"I don't think that's a good idea," said Ian. "It's late."

Petra's hands went icy. For an instant, she was at Joe Owens's house. Slick tile flooring underfoot, the air cool and dry... She heard gurgling. Was it Joe, struggling to breathe? There was something else. A remembered touch, like breath washing over her shoulder. Gooseflesh rose on her arms and the hair at the nape of her neck stood up. She turned quickly. Aside from Ian, she was alone.

"Are you okay?" he asked. "You went still all of a sudden."

"I..." She paused, trying to bring it all back. "I think I remember something about what happened at Joe's."

"What?"

"I remember being in the hall."

"And?" Ian coaxed.

"And there was something. A noise. Gurgling."

"Anything else?"

Petra shook her head.

"It's a good start," he said. "You'll remember more as time goes on."

"And I may not," she muttered.

He remained by the door. Even in the dark, she could sense his urgency—like the electricity of a lightning strike—in his need to leave, to hunt. "Give me two minutes to change," she said.

Ian moved farther into the corridor, as though backing away from her. "I still don't think it's a good idea that you come."

She reached for the lamp on the bedside table and flipped the switch. Light filled the room and she looked to the door. "I have to know what happened, Ian. So if you think you've discovered something that has to do with the attack on Joe, by all means, go after the clue. But I'm coming with you."

Ian followed the directions given by the GPS. Interstate. Frontage road. Finally, he turned onto a dirt track that headed straight toward the horizon. The sky, a velvety black full of diamonds, stretched on forever.

Their headlights cut through the night as the GPS continued to lead them onward. They crested a rise and began the descent. With the nose of the vehicle slowly tilting down, the headlights cast a wide arc, illuminating a pack of coyotes blocking their route. Petra gasped and reached for Ian at the same moment his foot slammed on the brake. The SUV jerked to a stop, kicking up a cloud of dust.

Slowly, the dirt settled, coating the hood and the windshield. Almost a dozen of the beasts sat on the shoulder of the road, their eyes reflecting the oncoming light. With a loping gait, the alpha male stood and slinked away, disappearing from view. The pack followed, leaving what had attracted the local wildlife in the first place.

Yuri Kuzntov.

Even from the driver's seat, Ian recognized him.

Petra sucked in a shaking breath. "Is that… Is he dead?"

Ian slid the gearshift into Park. "Wait here," he said, but Petra refused to stay back. She jumped out of the car and was at his side, her arms wrapped across her chest. What was her body language saying? That she needed warmth? Protection? Or to contain her emotions?

"I told you to wait in the car. You've seen enough already." Ian cast a glance at Kuzntov. "This isn't pretty and it sure as hell won't help you sleep better at night."

She pushed around him. "Is this the guy? Did he attack Joe?" And then she moaned, "Oh, God," and turned away.

Ian folded her into his arms. How many nights had he longed to hold her just once more? But not like this—not with a corpse just a few feet away, and not with Petra's freedom hanging in the balance. "Listen, get back in the car. I need to search this guy."

"Search him? He's dead."

"The dead tell the best stories." He gently pushed Petra toward his SUV. She didn't budge.

"I can help. I'm not feeble. You know that."

"I know you can take care of yourself. It's just…" What was it? What it always was, he supposed. "I'm trying to protect you."

"From a dead guy?"

"From whatever might really be going on here, and whatever it is you're caught up in."

"It'll be worse if I can't help. At least then I'll be… distracted a little."

Ian began to remind Petra that he worked better alone. But at the look on her face, he stopped. Realized that for two years, he'd been alone…and nothing about that time without her had been better. Not his work, and definitely not his personal life. "Okay, but only if you can handle it."

She swallowed. "I can handle it. But you never answered my question. Do you think that this guy attacked Joe?"

It was an interesting theory and Ian almost wanted to believe it himself—because if it was true, then Petra would be innocent. But he couldn't, not yet. Shaking his head, he said, "The timing's not quite right. The raid happened at five thirty this morning. Joe got a visitor around eight o'clock."

"That's two and a half hours," said Petra. "It'd give this guy time to get to Joe's place."

"In rush hour traffic, while trying to evade the police?" Ian shook his head. "Not bloody likely. No, as far as I've been able to see they communicated via text, and the last contact was ten days ago."

"He wasn't involved, then?"

"I didn't say that," said Ian. "I think he knew who attacked Joe, and why."

"Then who is he?" Petra asked. "And how did you find him?"

They approached the body and Ian knelt on the hard-packed ground. "This," he said, bending closer to examine the neck, "is Yuri Kuzntov. He's a Russian drug dealer who operates in Denver. And I found him because his name and number were on Joe Owens's contact list."

"Joe knew a drug dealer?"

Petra dropped down next to Ian, her knee brushing his thigh. His flesh sparked from the slight contact. Ian didn't care. He burned for her touch.

"Your client was looking for his special juice— provided by Yuri—about a week and a half ago. Any of this sound familiar?"

Petra shook her head. "Joe was a straight arrow. Until recently, at least."

"Maybe the drugs were new."

"It would explain the divorce and the erratic behavior. But Joe got randomly tested all the time and came back clean."

"Joe's tests weren't exactly random." Ian used air quotes around the word, as the headlights threw his shadow across the empty prairie.

"Hatch?" Petra guessed.

He nodded.

"I'd suspected, but you don't just accuse the owner of the Colorado Mustangs of tampering with the testing schedule without proof."

"I read Hatch's own words on the subject," Ian stated.

"What do you know? You have to tell me everything."

"First, I need to see what happened to Yuri here."

Petra scooted back, giving Ian as much light as the SUV's headlights provided. The coyotes had done a number on the throat, but still, the purple bruises around the neck were consistent with strangulation. The chest was bloodied and torn, but all those wounds appeared postmortem.

"He was choked to death and his body was dumped here." Ian patted down the front pockets of Yuri's jeans. Using finger and thumb, he pulled out a phone. With the toe of his boot, he rolled the Russian onto his stomach and checked the back pockets, as well. They were empty.

Ian stood and held his hand out to Petra. "I've seen all I need to. We can go."

She remained crouched on the ground. "Go? You're just going to leave him here?"

Ian scratched the side of his face. It was late. He wasn't in the mood for an argument. "Yuri Kuzntov was an evil man. He sold drugs. He was a human trafficker. I don't care if he rots or the coyotes come back and gnaw on his bones." He held up the phone. "This is what I care about."

Petra stood. "I'm not going anywhere until you call the police."

"No way," said Ian.

"You can't be that cruel."

Yes, Ian thought, he could. "Emergency services can track cellular calls. I don't want to use my phone to contact them about a homicide. They'll start asking questions that I don't intend to answer."

"Then use Yuri's phone."

It was a bad idea for the same reason, and yet... "If you insist that we call this in..."

"I insist."

"Come with me," Ian said. Suddenly, he was very tired and wanted nothing more than to sleep. To truly give up on his hunt. But he never would—not when Mateev was still out there somewhere.

Arms still folded over her chest, Petra stalked to the SUV and slid into the passenger seat. She slammed the door and watched Ian as he took his place behind the wheel. "You never did tell me how you found out all of this background about Yuri and Joe."

"Short answer?" Ian turned the vehicle around on the tight dirt track and began to drive. "In the age of the internet, nothing is secret."

"Long answer?"

"Another short answer—it's best if you don't know too much."

"But you think that this Yuri guy has something to do with the attack on Joe."

"Your client was in direct contact with some rough

people. The fact that he turned up brutalized doesn't surprise me."

Petra looked out the window and silently watched as the night folded around her.

"What are you thinking?" he asked.

"That I'm glad I came to you. It seems like everyone believes I'm guilty, except you."

"Everyone?" Ian asked. "Including you?"

"Like I said, I can't remember anything, so I don't know. And if I am guilty—"

"You aren't," said Ian, interrupting.

Petra began again. "And if I am, I want to know. I'll take full responsibility for my crimes."

"That's very honorable of you."

She shrugged. "Too many people get away with too much. I won't be one of them. It might keep me out of jail, but it would destroy my soul."

Ian was sure that jail would do a number on her soul as well, but he kept the comment to himself. Instead, he changed the subject. "I'll help you, Petra. I'm not sure what happened to Joe Owens, but there's enough about this scenario that I don't like," he said.

"Is it because my client was involved with the raid from this morning?" She paused. "Or I guess that was yesterday already."

The question was, could he really trust her with his ultimate goal—to kill Nikolai Mateev? Would she understand that the only way to stop Mateev was to end his life?

Those questions weren't hard to answer at all, and

Ian knew that he had to keep Petra ignorant of his true objective.

"You asked me for help," he said. "I'm willing to help. Besides, I'd never let you go to jail. Not if there was anything I could do to keep you out, at least."

He felt her gaze on him, warming his core and sending a bead of sweat trailing down his back.

"Because it's your job," she said.

What was it that she wanted him to say? "Because I care about you, Petra. Just because we aren't lovers anymore doesn't mean I don't give a damn."

They drove in silence as the endless grassland gave way to the frontage road they had taken earlier.

"Are you calling the police to report Yuri now?" she finally asked.

Ian said, "I'm not using my phone—or his phone, either."

"Then what are you going to do?"

From the darkness rose a light—a truck stop open twenty-four hours a day. "We'll stop here and buy a burner phone," Ian said. He quickly spotted the surveillance cameras and avoided driving directly through their vision. After parking at the side of the building, he turned to Petra. "Give me thirty seconds. I'll be right back."

Careful to keep his chin down and his face turned, he found a cheap phone with preprogrammed minutes. He paid with cash and was back in the car in a flash. He drove from the parking lot and pulled off to the side of the road.

After turning on the speaker function, Ian placed a call.

"Nine-one-one emergency dispatch. State the nature of your emergency."

Ian read off the GPS coordinates. "Go there and you'll find a body."

"Sir?" the dispatcher asked. "Can you repeat that, sir?"

Ian threw the phone out the window and sped into the night.

Petra snuggled into the passenger seat. Her jaw wasn't so tense and her eyes drifted slowly closed, only to be opened with the same languid motion. "Thanks for doing that. Calling in the body. Someone should know that he's out there."

"Someone does," said Ian. "Whoever strangled Yuri and then dumped his corpse."

"You know a lot about him," said Petra, her voice thick with exhaustion. "How?"

"He was part of a case I was working on this morning," said Ian. "We raided a house."

"Mmm-hmm," Petra murmured in the darkness. "I heard about that on the radio."

"It all goes back to my days with MI5. My first case, in fact."

"The one you were knighted for," she said.

"There's that tone again."

She gave him a small smile. "What happened?"

Everything. Nothing. Ian looked out the windshield, his jaw tight. The headlights stretched out in the distance. Denver International Airport rose up from the nothingness as a golden beacon, a lighthouse to a modern-day rocky coast.

What should he share with Petra? What should he conceal? He hadn't told his operatives everything about his plan—or really, anything. Then again, he didn't have feelings for them as he did— No. As he used to, for Petra.

He glanced in her direction. Her head was to the side, her eyes closed, and her long eyelashes kissed her cheeks. Her breathing was deep and rhythmic, her lips slightly parted. His own mouth burned with the memory of her kisses. He longed to touch her, to kiss her again. Yet he wouldn't; he'd sworn to himself he would never go down that road again.

Not even if she asked.

Chapter 6

The night had been too short. Once they returned to Ian's house, Petra had gotten a few hours of sleep and then risen, showered again, dressed in jeans and a wine-colored T-shirt.

She raked a hand through her still-damp hair and glanced at the blank TV screen. Her reflection stared back, and she turned away. She wanted to know what was being said about her—to find out if Joe was conscious or if the police had other suspects. But did she dare watch the news a second time?

She picked up the remote and pointed it at the TV. Her hand trembled as she pushed the power button. Immediately, a picture filled the screen. A reporter, microphone in hand, stood in front of a hospital entrance.

"This is Paul Sanchez," said the young reporter, "at Denver Area Medical Center. I just spoke to doctors about the most famous patient in the country, Mustangs quarterback Joe Owens.

"According to his attending physician, there has been no change since yesterday and the championship MVP is still unresponsive. As viewers know, Joe was brutally attacked in his home yesterday morning—stabbed seven times. The police have a person of interest."

Petra's face filled the screen. For a moment, she didn't recognize the woman in the photo—the dark circles around the eyes, the wild hair, the colorless lips, the smudge of blood on her cheek.

The picture made Petra look guilty—capable of trying to kill another person. She saw that fact herself. She pushed the power button again and the TV went black, and yet—the same face remained on the screen.

At eight o'clock, Petra and Ian were pulling out of his driveway. Ian had also donned a pair of jeans and a tightly fitted black T-shirt that accentuated his well-defined pecs and muscled arms.

She shivered with the memories of his strong arms encircling her waist, her breasts pressed against his hard chest. It wasn't just the physicality of their relationship she craved, but the safety of his embrace that she needed.

In a day that had the potential to be complicated, there was one issue Petra had to address. "How much will I owe you?" She tried to make light of the situation. "I know how much you make, and it's a lot."

Ian didn't reply, but he'd heard her. The question was impossible to miss.

His jaw tensed. "Petra, I won't take a cent from you."

She wanted to press, but also knew she'd never change Ian's mind. "Thanks," she said.

He nodded.

Petra searched for something to fill the silence. She had too much to say, and yet, would any of it matter?

"What now?" she asked.

"Last night, my research turned up some interesting facts. First, Arnie Hatch wanted to trade Joe Owens to the Kansas City Cyclones."

Even after all that had happened over the past twenty-four hours, that bit of information surprised Petra. "Really? Why would he want to get rid of Joe?"

"The excuse he gave had to do with a Canadian quarterback and the salary cap, but I don't buy it."

"And what happened to the offer?"

"The Cyclones weren't interested because of Joe's recent scandals, leaving Hatch with a player he didn't want."

"Not to beat the same drum, but why wouldn't Hatch want to keep the championship MVP? It makes no sense to me. Joe was a hard worker and made the plays that counted."

"Actually, there's more to this saga. The rumors about Hatch and Joe's wife are true—and they're pretty serious. Larissa lives in a penthouse that Hatch pays for."

That was also news to Petra. "Which means what?"

"That Arnie Hatch had every reason in the world to want Joe dead."

"Do you think Hatch tried to kill Joe?"

Ian shook his head as he veered his car into the exit lane. "I doubt it. But I wouldn't put it past him to hire someone to take care of a problem."

Was her case going to be solved so simply? Jealousy, lust and greed; had Arnie Hatch decided to dispatch his team's biggest star—who also happened to be his biggest personal problem? "And you have evidence proving Hatch was involved?"

He pulled up at a stoplight. "That's just it—I don't. There has to be something, but he hasn't communicated about it electronically. Which shows he's at least *that* intelligent."

"And what about the dead Russian?"

"I'm not sure how he fits into this, either."

Ian's answers were far from satisfying. "So where does that leave us?"

"We're going to investigate things the old-fashioned way. There are a few people we need to talk to." After pulling in to the parking lot of an expensive high-rise building, Ian turned off the engine. "And we're going to start with Larissa Owens."

Petra's mouth went dry. Larissa was far from being her friend, but they were friendly—or had been when the marriage and the career were good.

How would she react to seeing Petra in her home? Would she wonder why she was out on bail instead of sitting in a prison cell? Petra didn't know for sure, but could guess that her reception wasn't going to be good.

A uniformed doorman greeted them in the lobby. "Can I help you?" he asked, solicitous and serious at the same time.

"I need to see Larissa Owens," said Ian. "Tell her it's regarding Joe Owens and Petra Sloane."

The doorman eyed Petra warily and she wondered if he recognized her from the constant media coverage. No doubt she'd become Denver's most notorious citizen. She felt the walls closing in, trapping her in a continual loop of bad press.

The doorman picked up a house phone and spoke softly into the receiver. He placed the phone back on its base. "She said you can come up." He held out a keycard. "You'll need this to access the top floor."

A set of gilded elevator doors opened, and they stepped inside the car. Ian waved the keycard over the reader and the doors slid closed.

"That was easier than I thought it would be," said Petra, as the elevator began its ascent. "Larissa could have refused to let us into her home, if she wanted. It makes me think she's got nothing to hide."

"Or she has everything to hide and is hoping that by being helpful, she won't be implicated," he said.

The elevator doors slid open to reveal a living room that was decorated in white and silver. The far wall was a bank of windows overlooking the Denver skyline and the Rocky Mountains beyond. Understated. Elegant. Impressive.

Larissa Owens rose from a white leather sofa as

Ian and Petra stepped off the elevator. A former Miss New Mexico, Larissa stood a touch under five feet ten inches tall. Black hair fell to her shoulders in a blunt cut with a fringe of bangs. Without question, she looked like a modern-day Cleopatra in leggings and expensive sandals.

"Petra," she said, her hands outstretched. "Thank you for stopping by. This is all tragic, just so tragic."

Petra clasped hands with the other woman. "Thank you for seeing me. This is my friend Ian Wallace. He owns a private security firm and is helping me look into what really happened to Joe." *And to clear my name*, she said to herself.

"I heard on the news that you'd been named as a person of interest. I told Arnie that I didn't believe a word of it." She sighed a little too heavily for Petra to see it as anything other than an act.

"I was just about to have some breakfast," Larissa said. "Have you eaten yet? I can have the chef prepare something for you."

"Actually," Ian said, "we came to ask a few questions, if you wouldn't mind? I know this is a…difficult time."

"Sure," she said. She walked back to the leather sofa and sat. Indicating two chairs, she said, "Sit, please."

Petra's spine was stiff and her pulse raced. Yet she took a seat without comment, perching on the edge of the chair. The scenario became an even greater puzzle to Petra now. Had Larissa been so dissatisfied with Joe's income that she went after his boss? Killing him would really have been the only way to get free, given that Joe wasn't keen on a divorce, and Larissa would have been stuck in limbo.

Or…could she have played an even larger role? Petra wondered if Larissa had a big life insurance policy on Joe. Anger and indignation began to burn in her stomach.

"When did you hire a chef?" she asked.

"When I moved out." Larissa said. "Why do you want to know?"

"We don't. Can I ask you where you were from eight o'clock to nine o'clock yesterday morning?" Ian said as he sat.

"Me?" Larissa placed a perfectly manicured hand on her chest. "I was home with the girls until eight thirty. That's when they catch the bus to school."

"And where's the bus stop?"

"By the front door."

"And you walk them downstairs yourself?" Ian asked.

"I can see where this is going," said Larissa. "To clear Petra of the charges, you have to find another suspect. No one is more convenient than Joe's estranged wife."

"With all due respect," said Petra, "you haven't answered the question."

"With all due respect," Larissa snapped, "I don't have to. You aren't the police. I'm under no obligation to talk to you."

"Why let us up here at all, Larissa?" Petra asked. "You must have guessed why we'd stopped by. Was it to make yourself look innocent by helping? Face it—you have a reason for wanting Joe dead."

"Your temerity astounds me, Petra." Larissa stood. "Why would I want to hurt Joe?"

"A private chef? A penthouse apartment? You need more money than Joe's salary."

"Joe is the father of my children. I care about him and would rather see him alive than dead."

Petra said, "I don't believe a word of what you're saying, Larissa. You have obviously moved on to bigger and better bank accounts."

"I loved Joe, but recently—he'd changed. I went to Arnie with my concerns and things progressed." Larissa gave a little shrug. "Arnie's a good man—and stable. It's what I need right now. I'm comfortable with the way things are and not interested in another marriage. Neither is he."

Petra felt as if she'd backed into a corner and couldn't find a way to escape. She glanced at Ian.

"I assume that there's video surveillance in this building. Something that proves you were in your apartment yesterday morning?" Ian asked.

"I assume so," said Larissa. "I'll call down to the lobby and ask that the doorman cooperate."

Petra wasn't ready to give up so easily. "Just because you were home doesn't mean you weren't involved. You could have paid someone to attack Joe."

Larissa sighed. "I let you into my home so you'd take me off your list of possible suspects, but, Petra, I didn't try to kill Joe. And for what it's worth I don't think you did, either."

With a sigh of her own, Petra asked, "What do you think happened?"

"To be honest, I don't know."

Ian stood. "If you think of anything, please let us know."

"Of course," she said. She moved to the elevator and pushed the call button. The doors slid open. "I'll phone down and ask that the doorman make yesterday morning's video available to you."

Petra stood, suddenly tired, even though it wasn't yet nine in the morning. "Thanks," she said, as she stepped into the elevator.

Ian followed and the doors closed.

"Do you believe Larissa?" he asked.

Petra paused. "Actually, I do."

"So do I."

"Which leaves us where?"

"Down by one suspect."

"You still haven't considered one possible option, Ian. I might be guilty."

"You're right," he said. "I haven't."

Petra swallowed. "There was a psychologist on the news last night. He said I was rage filled and my attack on Joe was triggered by an event. Don't you get it? He might be right."

Ian stroked the side of his face. "You can't believe everything you see on TV. Besides, we still haven't talked to Arnie Hatch and we don't know how Yuri Kuzntov's death plays into all of this."

"What if it doesn't?" Petra asked. "What if the

dead Russian and my client have nothing to do with one another?"

"They're connected," said Ian. He strode through the lobby, his part of the conversation obviously finished.

And yet she couldn't shake the feeling that there was more going on. There was something Ian wasn't telling her. It meant there was only one question that mattered to her—whether she could really rely on him or not.

The white bowl that was Denver City Stadium rose out of the skyscrapers of the downtown. They pulled in to the parking lot. Acres of blacktop meant for thousands and thousands of football fans on game day spread out around them. Most of the spaces were empty and Ian chose one near the door.

He cut the engine and turned to Petra. "Are you ready?" he asked.

"No," she said. She gave him a wan smile. "But let's go."

Without another word, they walked to the front door. A security guard sitting behind a long desk asked, "Can I help you?"

"We're here to see Arnie Hatch," Ian said.

The guard looked at Petra and narrowed his eyes. Ian could tell that he recognized her from the unrelenting media coverage surrounding Joe Owens's attack—and more than that, he believed Petra to be guilty. Ian stepped forward, shielding her from the man's glare.

"Do you have an appointment?" the guard asked.

"We do not," said Ian.

"Mr. Hatch doesn't have any time in his schedule today."

"Tell him it's regarding Joe Owens."

The guard grunted. "I imagine it is."

"I want to ask him about his plans, since Kansas City turned down the deal to trade Joe Owens. Was murder the contingency to get rid of a player he no longer wanted?"

The guard stared openmouthed at Ian.

"Go ahead," Ian taunted. "Pick up the phone and ask him. He's not busy right now. He doesn't have an appointment until half past ten."

The guard snatched up a phone and spoke softly into the receiver. After a moment, he turned to Ian and Petra. "Mr. Hatch can meet with you for five minutes," he said. "Take the second elevator on the left."

They approached and the elevator doors opened. There were no control buttons, but the door slid shut as soon as they stepped on and the car began to ascend. The doors opened to the same office Ian had seen on the Mustangs' website the night before. Hatch sat behind the same desk. Today he wore a golf shirt with a Mustangs logo and a large gold wristwatch. He didn't look up as they approached.

"Mind if we have a seat?" Ian asked, unwilling to let him set the terms of their meeting. "Ask you a few questions?"

"Do what you want," said Hatch. "It's your four minutes and forty-five seconds."

Ian immediately understood Arnie Hatch. Mistrustful by nature, Hatch needed to believe that he was in charge and that all his secrets were safe.

Ian waited until Petra took a high-backed leather chair that faced the desk, then took an identical seat next to her. She began, "I won't waste time with small talk, then. What do you think happened to Joe Owens?"

"Are you serious? This *is* a waste of my time," said Hatch. "The cops found you at Joe's house, Ms. Sloane, covered in blood. It seems I don't have to think too much since you tried to kill Joe because you couldn't control him and you were going to lose your job."

"And Joe's erratic behavior never bothered you?" she asked.

Hatch shrugged. "I've been in business a long time. If you're successful, there's pressure. Eventually, most everyone cracks, and people act out in strange ways. Joe. You."

"But not you?" Ian asked.

"I said most everyone, not everyone."

"And yet you wanted to get rid of Joe." Ian continued, setting the trap about the hacked email. "According to you, he was a liability."

Hatch's eyes widened a little. "I don't know what you're talking about. Joe was last year's championship MVP."

"But endorsements were less than you expected," said Ian. "The team in Kansas City didn't want him.

Hell, he wouldn't even give your girlfriend the divorce she wanted—and that's when you told your coach that Owens was a liability you wanted gone. You also had a plan for dealing with him. Maybe you carried that plan out."

Arnie slapped an open palm on his desk. "I don't know where you got your so-called information, but it's all a damned lie."

"You and I both know every word I just said was true, and the police will be more than a little interested in speaking to you about the fact a player you saw as troublesome is now in the hospital."

Hatch cursed and wiped the back of his neck. "We don't need to get the police involved. I can explain everything, but if you breathe one word of this to the authorities, I'll sue you for libel—draining every cent you have in court costs. I did want to trade Joe. On the field he was fine, but sponsors didn't like him. He wasn't charming on camera. I wanted someone who was marketable."

"So, you didn't want to keep Joe because he couldn't sell aftershave even though you hired him to play football," said Petra, not bothering to keep the sarcasm from her voice.

"Don't act like you don't understand the business," said Hatch. "Professional sports is as much about the media as it is the game."

"Don't scold me, Hatch. Even with Joe in the hospital, he's still my client and it's my job—my duty—to protect his interests."

"Then as his agent you know Owens had a rough

off-season. Larissa left with the kids and filed for divorce, which led to partying and other things that the organization wanted to keep quiet. Like I said, he cracked. I wanted him gone before he took down the whole team."

"And speaking of his divorce, you have a personal interest in seeing that go through," said Ian.

Hatch waved Ian's comment away. "That old rumor? There's nothing to it."

"We've spoken to Larissa," said Petra. "You've provided her with a very nice penthouse. You must care for her a lot. Wanting to be with her is reason enough to want Joe gone—and in a place farther away than Kansas City."

With a sigh, Hatch said, "Larissa Owens is a nice lady and I enjoy her company. But I have more ex-wives than I care to count and don't need another one." He looked at the watch on his wrist. "Your time's up."

"I'm not going anywhere, Hatch," said Petra. "There's a lot more you need to explain—like why you continually tested my client for drugs."

Ian admired Petra's spirit, but they'd gotten what they came for and it was time to go. He stood. "Our time's up, Petra."

"Wh-what?" she spluttered.

"Let's go."

With a pen in his hand, Hatch returned his attention to the papers on his desk and Petra got slowly to her feet.

"One last thing," said Ian. "Do you know a man named Yuri Kuzntov?"

Arnie quit writing. "No," he said without looking up.

Bingo.

As before, the doors opened without pressing a call button. They stepped on without comment. As the doors closed, Petra rounded on Ian.

"What the hell is the matter with you? We need to talk to Arnie Hatch some more. There are too many parts of his story that don't make sense."

"That's because he's lying," said Ian. "Hatch knows something about what happened to Joe."

Petra loosened her folded arms and let them hang at her sides. "How can you tell?"

"He went on the offensive when I told him that we knew about him wanting to trade Joe. Honest people might not own up to the truth right away, but when they know their secret's out they stop the ruse. Guilty people get indignant."

"He confessed to having an affair with Larissa right away," Petra said.

"Exactly," Ian stated. "And he threatened to sue me if I discussed his issues with Joe."

"I hope you're right," said Petra. "Because if I just helped you accuse Arnie Hatch of trying to kill Joe Owens, and we're wrong, I'll never work as a sports agent in Denver—or anywhere else—again."

Ian didn't bother reminding her that unless they found someone else to blame for Joe's attack, she'd be in jail and her career prospects were the last thing she'd be worrying about. Then again, he didn't have to. Petra was a smart woman; she already knew.

"What do we do now? Go to the police?" she asked. "I'm sure Hatch's threat about a lawsuit didn't scare you."

Ian shook his head. "Nothing about that man is frightening. Hatch has more secrets. Now all we have to do is find them. I'd like to get a look at his phone records. Maybe there's something connecting him to Yuri. Either way, once we have real proof, I'll send a report to your lawyer."

The elevator let them off in the lobby and together they walked to Ian's SUV. The sun was high in the sky and already the temperature was climbing.

Ian started the engine with the key fob as a red sedan pulled up next to them. The window lowered and a man in his forties leaned on the sill. He had dark hair and a thin face, but most noticeable was that both his eyes had been blackened. His bottom lip was split and a red welt bloomed on his cheek.

"Petra?" the man said.

"Rick? You look awful. What happened?"

"There was a distracted driver on Interstate 23 yesterday morning," he said. "She slammed into my car, shoving me into another lane. My car was totaled and aside from the fact that I don't like the loaner I'm driving, I'm okay." He paused. "Listen, I heard what happened yesterday. I'm sorry. I tried to call…"

"I lost my phone, you know, at Joe's."

"That's awful. The news is saying that you don't remember anything."

"Bits and pieces," said Petra, "but nothing helpful."

"It might be shock."

She gave a small shrug. "I had one of my headaches," she said.

Jealousy, hot and acidic, flooded through Ian's chest. Who was this guy—and who was he to Petra? It was clear that she had shared her secrets with him.

"Petra," Ian said. His voice had a hard bite. "We need to go."

"Go where?" Rick asked, like he somehow had a right to know. Ian's hands and feet went cold. His chest constricted. What if this guy did have a right? What if he was more to Petra than a nosy friend?

"Rick, this is Ian Wallace. He's helping me figure out what happened with Joe. Ian, this is Richard Albright, the team doctor."

Team doctor? Well, maybe Rick could be helpful, after all. "Have you noticed any changes in Joe Owens lately?"

"I really can't discuss the players. Confidentiality and all."

Ian grunted. Some friend. "Anything you can tell me, that might help me clear Petra?"

Albright turned off the ignition and withdrew the key. He held it in his hand, as if trying to guess its weight. "I saw a clip on the news. It made it look like Luis Martinez was involved with the case."

Ian lifted an eyebrow. According to Petra, Detective Sergeant Luis Martinez was more than involved in the case, he was the lead investigator. "Why's that an issue?"

"He's friends with Joe," said Albright.

A cop investigating a crime where he personally knew the victim wasn't ideal. But as a police officer, you took the calls you got. Then again, any personal relationship could taint the investigation. "How well did they know each other?"

"By my estimation, they were good friends. Joe and Luis grew up together and even played on the same high school team. Joe got a university scholarship and was drafted into the pros. Luis went to community college and joined the police force afterward. I thought it was nice that they stayed close—it's not always like that when folks get famous, you know."

Petra turned to Ian. "I remember thinking that Martinez was presumptuous when he referred to Joe by his first name. It seemed incredibly familiar. I guess it really was."

It was more than odd. It was wrong, so wrong that Ian's list of suspects grew by one. "Thanks for the tip," he said to Rick. "But we really do have some leads to run down."

With his hand on Petra's elbow, Ian led her to the passenger seat of the car. Once in the driver's seat, he pulled out his phone and opened the internet app. With the engine idling and the auto in park, he searched the Colorado Highway Patrol's blotter. There, on the first page, was an accident involving Dr.

Richard Albright and a distracted driver. Ian closed the search, slightly dissatisfied.

"How well do you know Dr. Albright?" he asked, then ground his teeth together, angry that he cared at all.

He slammed the gearshift into Drive and dropped his foot on the accelerator. The large auto shot forward and he eased up on the gas.

"Really, it's not any of your business," said Petra.

"So you aren't going to answer my question?"

She looked out the window. "I don't know what you want me to say."

"Listen, I'm helping you not because I'm a nice guy but…" He paused. "I'm helping you to honor what we used to be. So, yeah, I suppose you do owe me the truth."

"If you're jealous, don't be. Rick Albright is a nice guy, but I never mix business with pleasure."

"I'm not jealous." Even Ian heard the grumble in his voice.

Ian reminded himself that Petra had plenty of friends he'd never met. She lived in a condo he'd never seen. She slept in a bed he'd never touched. Petra had moved on. He had no choice but to accept it. He refused to embarrass himself anymore and turned on the radio.

"In local news," said the announcer. "Sports agent Petra Sloane has been named as a person of interest in the attempted murder of her client Joe Owens."

"Damn it," he said as he hit the power button, silencing the radio. "Sorry about that."

"The story is everywhere," she said. "I doubt there's anyone in Denver who hasn't heard—and doesn't think I'm guilty."

Even if Petra was right, it was Ian's job to prove them all wrong—and prove her innocence.

Chapter 7

Petra sat in the passenger seat while Ian drove. Silence was a barrier, pressing them down and keeping them apart. He hadn't even mentioned their destination, yet Petra had guessed. They were headed to the first safe house RMJ established.

Petra recalled the day that Ian had purchased the property. Working as legal counsel, she'd opened an LLC and attended the Realtor's meeting for her unnamed client. Then, with keys in hand, she and Ian had met at the small home.

They toured the property as Ian regaled her with his plans for the future.

"This," he said, as they stopped in what had been a back bedroom, "is where the super-computer will be housed. It's happening, Petra. Rocky Mountain

Justice is coming together. I'll make a life for us, one that you deserve."

His excitement was palpable. The hairs at the nape of her neck stood on end.

She moved to a window and looked out, trying to see the future he envisioned. It was mid-February. A blizzard had descended on the city. The snow was so thick that Petra could hardly see across the street. The window reflected the room behind her. Empty spaces. Recessed lights. Ian. Her own reflection. She watched as he touched her.

He reached for her hair, tangling his fingers into her locks. Lifting her tresses, he kissed the back of her neck lightly—like a single snowflake falling onto the petal of a rose.

His fingers moved from her shoulders to her arms. They held hands. His front was pressed to her back. "We ought to christen the safehouse, don't you think?"

She grew damp with desire. "Of course," she purred. "We wouldn't want our space to belong to someone else."

He rocked his hips against her. He was hard. She knew he would be.

Palms splayed on the window glass, Petra braced herself. Ian lifted her skirt. She recalled the chill of her exposed thighs as his hands blazed a trail over her skin. He slid a finger inside her, igniting her passion completely.

He traced her lips with his wet finger. She licked away the taste of her desire and he kissed her again.

Ian entered her from behind, taking her hard and fast. Petra came at once, the sensation so intense it had left her weak in the knees. He shouted her name, shaking with the power of his own passion, holding on to her as he shuddered with completion. Eventually, they separated and Petra stood straight, reassembling her clothes. Her palm prints had remained on the glass...

She returned to the present, the feeling of Ian inside her as real as the sun that now shone on her face. Petra flushed at the recollection.

She gave him a sideways glance. He regarded her quickly before returning his gaze to the road.

Her blush deepened and heat climbed up her cheeks. "I remember when we bought the house."

"So do I," he said.

Again Petra found herself trying to read his comment. There was nothing in either his words or tone that clued her in to his thoughts or feelings.

"We had lots of dreams and plans back then," he said as he eased the SUV next to the curb.

"Too bad they never came true," she said.

"It wasn't that bad," said Ian. "Was it?"

"We broke up and haven't spoken for more than two years. I'd say it wasn't good."

Ian edged into a parking space marked as reserved. "No regrets for moving on, then?"

"Regrets," she echoed with a short laugh. "I've never loved anyone in my life the way I love you."

"Loved?" he asked. "Or love?"

Petra's breath caught in her chest. She'd been such a fool to rush to Ian.

It wasn't simply that she was in a mess, nor that he was well equipped to help her. It was that she wanted back what she had lost—the life they'd shared. And here they were—but it was nothing like she hoped.

His question still hung in the air, like a cartoon speech bubble with a trail of dots. Loved or love?

"Both," she said, finally answering. "Neither."

The car stilled as Ian turned off the engine. She opened the door and oven-like heat rolled off the road. At the front door, Ian pressed his thumb to what appeared to be a doorbell. But his thumbprint had activated a keypad hidden in the home's facade. Ian entered a seven-digit code.

The panel slid back into place and there was a soft click as the door was automatically unlocked. Ian pulled the door open.

"After you," he said.

What had once been a typical entryway, tiled in cream linoleum, was now a white-paneled chamber. The door to the outside closed and locked, trapping them in a square of white.

The secure and futuristic space left Petra slightly uneasy. An electronic female voice came from hidden speakers. "Name?"

"Ian Wallace and approved visitor, Petra Sloane."

Ian's face appeared on the wall in front of them. More than two-dozen red dots filled his likeness.

"Vocal and facial scan complete," said the voice. There was another click, and a door slid open.

"Follow me," said Ian.

The entire house had been gutted and turned into

a single room. More than a dozen large screens filled the wall opposite the door. They were all ablaze with pictures and light. A battle that raged in a desert somewhere. A constantly rotating view from London street cameras. A static picture of the red-walled Kremlin.

Two rows of tables stretched across the room. Each table held more than a dozen monitors. All of them were filled with computer code. None were manned.

"I like what you've done with the place," she said. But the comment was for Ian's benefit, not hers. Seeing the refurbished safe house filled her not with pride, but misery. From the beginning, this had been her dream, too.

"If the 16th Street Mall offices used to be the face of Rocky Mountain Justice," said Ian, "this safe house was the brain."

"I guess it is," said Petra, as awe in what Ian had created began to take over. "I'm not sure if I'm trapped in a sci-fi movie or a military thriller, but this is all…" She paused, not sure how to finish her sentence.

"Impressive?" asked a woman.

Petra turned to the voice. Ian's longtime communications specialist and Petra's former friend, Katarina, stood in the back of the room. With all the monitors, she'd missed her onetime companion.

Kat wore her dark hair long. The few streaks of gray that lightened her locks made her look all the more worldly and confident.

"Kat. Look at you, you look great."

"Petra…" Kat moved forward and wrapped her arms around Petra's shoulders, pulling her into a hug. "It's so good to see you."

Petra returned the embrace. "I didn't expect to see you here. Ian said that RMJ was closed."

"We've collected quite a bit of information over the years," said Kat. "It's going to take some time to destroy it all. I have to say, I'm surprised to see you both at the safe house."

"I'm helping Petra," he said. "And I wanted to check on a few things."

"You're in good hands, then, Petra—but you know that. Ian'll help you clear up this Joe Owens mess."

That's what Petra had been hoping. Yet they'd spent the morning trying to find someone else who might be responsible for the attack on Joe and had nothing.

"Thanks," said Petra with a wan smile. She couldn't help but wonder what Kat had heard on the news. Or worse yet, what she believed. Was her old friend like everyone else? Did she see Petra as a killer?

"This way," said Ian, pointing in the direction Kat had been.

She saw it then, a door, that led to an office. A large wooden desk sat in the middle of the cramped room. Papers in neat stacks stood along one edge of the desk and a computer filled another.

Petra leaned against a wall and watched Ian take a seat behind the desk and power up the computer.

"It was nice to see Kat again," she said. "How's everyone else at RMJ? Julia? Roman?"

Ian tapped on the keyboard as he spoke. "Julia's fine, I suppose. Roman's pissed at me for closing shop."

"I saw that he got married."

Ian looked up from the computer, one eyebrow lifted. "Oh?"

The intensity of his stare pinned Petra to the wall. She felt exposed and at the same time, truly seen. There was a tightening deep in her belly, and her palms tingled with the need to touch him.

She swallowed. "Kat posted pictures to social media. Don't worry, only her friends can see her page. Roman's new wife is pretty. Do you like her?"

"Madelyn's great. She's a medical student." Ian's gaze returned to the computer. "And pregnant."

"Roman, a dad? That is shocking." She paused. "No wonder he's mad about RMJ closing. It's never great timing to lose a job, but it's especially hard when there's a baby on the way."

"He's employable," said Ian. "He'll find something else."

Now it was Petra's turn to get angry. "Is that how you really feel? I thought that RMJ was more to you than just a job. I thought it was a calling—something that you'd sacrifice everything to make succeed." Obviously, she was talking about her, about their relationship. She didn't want it to be so personal and spoke again. "More than that, wasn't it you who never hired people, only brought someone new into your family?"

"I have enough to worry about in my own life not to complicate it with someone else's," he said.

Petra moved to the desk and stood directly in front of Ian. "Is it always easy for you? Being so laser focused? You never have to worry about anything else because you always have a single priority."

Ian shook his head. "Once I've made up my mind to get something done I can't think of anything else. My goal is always with me. It keeps me awake at night, and when I do sleep, it's in my dreams." He hesitated. "It sounds bloody awful, but it's the only way to hit the target we're paid to seek. The only way to do this job."

Petra looked away. "It does sound bloody awful."

Ian opened his desk drawer, pulled out a smartphone and handed it to her. "You can use this until you have time to get a new phone." He gave her the unlock code and added, "This is an extra for RMJ. I guess we won't need it anymore, so take your time,"

"Thanks," she said. "I need to check in with work. Do you mind?"

"Of course not," said Ian as he stood. "I expected as much. Besides, I need to speak with Kat and that'll give you a moment of privacy."

Petra waited until Ian left the room and then sat on the edge of the desk. She wiped her wet palms on her thighs and entered her boss's direct number. The phone rang several times before it was answered. "This is Mike Dawson."

"Mike," she said. Her pulse raced and her voice was a little breathless. "It's Petra."

Silence stretched out. "What do you want?"

Well, this was not going well from the start. "I thought I should check in, see how work's going."

Another silence. "I sent you an email this morning. Haven't you seen it?"

"I haven't had time to get on a computer..." she began.

Mike interrupted. "I terminated your employment. We can't be associated with you."

She pressed her eyes shut. Hot tears collected on her lashes, yet they didn't fall. "I see," she said. There was nothing else to say, not really. "Okay."

"And Petra?"

"Yes?"

"Don't call here again."

She hung up before Mike had a chance to end the call. Petra pressed a knuckle to her lips. Inhale. One. Two. Three. Exhale.

Ian stood at the doorway. "Not good?" he asked.

"I've been let go from the agency," she said with a shake of her head.

"That's tough," said Ian.

"I don't know what I'm going to do now. My reputation is in tatters. Even if I somehow stay out of jail, I'll never work as an agent again. Who would be crazy enough to hire me?"

"You'll figure something out."

Petra was too filled with venom for his platitudes. "You mean like Roman will find a new job?"

"I'm not going to argue with you about my decision to close RMJ," he said. "We lost a contract with the FBI. That's a big deal."

"Just like there are other jobs out there, there's other clients for Rocky Mountain Justice."

"No," said Ian, "Not really."

"I don't get you. It's not like you to quit."

Ian's jaw flexed. She held her breath, waiting for him to say something—admit what was really going on. He didn't.

After brushing past Petra, Ian dropped into the seat behind the desk and began to tap on the keyboard of his computer. "I'm not quitting on you," he said. "Not until we find out how Luis Martinez is connected to what happened to Joe Owens."

Petra moved behind the desk and looked at the screen over Ian's shoulder. He'd brought up the Denver Police Department's online database. Petra read along as Ian found the personnel page for Luis Martinez. Martinez was listed as single, Roman Catholic and assigned to the Cherry Creek precinct. "Exactly what do you plan to do with this information?"

Ian shrugged and leaned back, chin in hand. "Not sure yet. Depends on how it meshes with everything we've uncovered so far." Pointing at the screen, he said, "See this? Owens lives in Belcaro, right? That's not the same precinct Martinez is assigned to."

"Sure," said Petra, "but they're close."

"An APB probably went out over the radio with the home alarm. Then whoever was in the area responded." Ian exhaled and leaned back in his seat.

"Couldn't he have been out on another assignment, something that brought him to Belcaro?"

"Maybe."

After tapping a few more keys, Martinez's bank account filled the screen. Petra's eye was drawn to a single line. It was a deposit from three days prior for ten thousand dollars. "That's not right," she said.

Ian brought up an electronic copy of the check. The image was pixelated, and yet the name, address and signature were all unmistakable. For some reason, Joe Owens had given Martinez a large amount of money.

Petra wrapped her arms over her chest, holding tight. Excitement? Fear? "What was Joe doing writing a check to Luis Martinez?" she asked, a quiver in her voice.

"If my guess is right," said Ian, "your client was being blackmailed."

"Then why would Martinez want Joe dead? Wouldn't he be happy with the easy money?"

"Unless Joe was tired of paying. You said yourself that something had happened, and Joe wanted you to handle the PR. What if Joe was going to tell the world that he'd been blackmailed by a Denver cop."

"It means," said Petra, "that Martinez has all the reason in the world to want Joe Owens dead."

Ian sat behind the desk with the phone to his ear and watched Petra pace the length of the small office.

"Thank you," he said into the receiver, before adding, "Tell him I'll be there in thirty minutes."

He hung up the phone. Petra stopped pacing.

"And?" she asked.

"I spoke to a contact I have in the Denver PD. He got in touch with Martinez. Martinez is willing to meet with us, if we can get to the hospital ASAP."

Petra lifted her eyebrows. "Really?"

Ian was on his feet. He handed Petra her bag. "Let's go. I want a chance to talk to Martinez in some place neutral. If he's at the police station, we'll never get an honest answer."

In less than half an hour, Ian and Petra walked through the front doors of the Denver Area Medical Center, a sprawling complex of concrete and glass. The medicinal scent of antiseptic hung in the air. Voices carried over a PA system, nothing more than noise to his ears.

Signs led them to the cafeteria and Ian paused at the door. Bright light shone through a series of skylights and reflected off the empty tables. Martinez, a large man with broad shoulders and short dark hair, sat alone and was easy to spot.

The cop lifted his chin in greeting and stood as they approached. "You must be Ian Wallace," he said. "I'm Detective Sergeant Luis Martinez. You said you have some information about the Owens's case?"

"We do," said Ian.

"Have a seat," Martinez said, amiably enough. "I'd offer to buy you a coffee, but it's really bad." As if to prove his point, he took a sip and grimaced. "It might lead to a complaint of police brutality."

Ian pulled out a chair for Petra. As she sat, he said, "We're fine, but we need to talk, and we don't have a lot of time." Ian took his own seat. "There's a question about one of the last checks Joe Owens wrote…"

Martinez shifted in his seat, staring at the cup he held. "I don't know what you're talking about."

It was an obvious lie. "Let's not play games. I've seen the check. Ten thousand dollars must be a lot of money for a cop like you."

"What do you want me to say?"

"Start with the truth," Petra suggested.

"I didn't try to kill Joe, if that's what you're insinuating."

Ian said, "There's a lot of evidence that says otherwise."

"Like what?" Martinez asked.

"Like why were you the first to arrive at Joe Owens's house as soon as the alarm started going off. It's almost like you were waiting nearby," said Petra.

Martinez dropped his gaze to his cup. "Joe was my best friend when we were kids—like a brother, really. We grew apart when he got the big scholarship and went away to school. Then he came back to Denver and was the hometown hero. He used to invite me over to play poker once a week, but that stopped a while back." Martinez let out a long sigh and slumped back. The chair groaned in protest.

The other man was in emotional pain, that much was obvious. Yet was it real? Or was he putting on a performance for their benefit? Ian was eager to gauge Martinez's reaction and see if it gelled with his most recent theory. "Is that why you blackmailed Joe? Because he was a nice guy, and therefore an easy mark?"

Martinez looked up. His eyes flashed with anger and indignation. "You have it all wrong. I was on my way to Joe's just to see him and hang out when the dispatch came through. I was the closest one, so I happened to arrive first. The rest of the case unfolded just as I reported."

"And the fact that you were friends?"

"I'm a professional and know how to do my job. But it's a small world. Sometimes cases are a little personal."

"And the money?" Petra asked. "We saw the check Joe gave you."

Martinez sagged even farther. "In college, I developed a bit of a gambling habit," he said.

Ian could see the rest of the scenario without Martinez saying a word. "You mean you've become addicted to gambling."

The detective nodded slowly. The man was unquestionably dejected. Ian almost felt sorry for him. Almost, but not entirely. "Go on," he ordered.

"I got in debt. Then borrowed some to pay that off. Lost more. More debt. It kinda got out of hand."

"And good guy that Joe Owens was, he bailed you out. You're a cop, right?" Ian pressed. "You can't be indebted to unscrupulous people."

Martinez shrugged. "Something like that."

Ian was close to getting a confession. The scent hovered in the air—a miasma of sweat and stale coffee and desperation. "More than that, your friend got famous and filthy rich. And you got stuck working for the PD. It's a thankless job for very little pay."

"It's not like that," said Martinez.

Ian wasn't in the mood for the other man's excuses. "You needed more money and asked Joe, and when he turned you down, things got heated. You didn't mean to hurt him, but you did, and then you panicked and left. When Petra showed up, you got an idea."

Martinez's spine went rigid. He sat taller. "I'm telling you that's not what happened," he said.

"But I'm close."

"Not at all. Joe wouldn't just give me the money. I had to attend Gamblers Anonymous meetings before he paid a dime. Anyway, I went to a few meetings, just to get the money. Then, even though I didn't need to, I went to a meeting the other morning before my shift. The program clicked for me and I understood my problem. I headed to Joe's to thank him for forcing me to do right. I was already in the neighborhood when I heard the APB."

Ian wasn't sure if he believed Martinez. It would be easy to prove his alibi—or not. But another thought came to him. One that was almost as good as a complete confession. "Your carelessness has tainted every bit of evidence collected at the scene."

Martinez held his hands open, palms up. "I screwed up, man. What do you want me to say?"

"That you targeted me and ruined my life to keep your gambling secret safe," said Petra, her eyes flashing with anger.

"I'm sorry for the way things went down, really I am," said Martinez.

"Sorry?" Petra leaned forward. "Sorry doesn't cut

it. The story of how I allegedly attacked Joe is all over the news. I lost my job and I'll never work as an agent again."

"Another detective would've found the same evidence as me."

Petra gave a derisive snort.

"You need to come clean, Martinez," said Ian. "Assuming that you aren't the actual culprit, you never should have named Petra as a person of interest. You need to get in front of a judge and make this right."

Martinez picked up his coffee and took a swig. His throat worked, long after the swallow ended. "Joe, he wanted to be the big football star, and he was—is. Me, I only wanted to serve and protect." He took another sip of coffee and looked away.

Just then a hospital security guard approached. "Are you Detective Sergeant Martinez?" he asked.

Martinez nodded.

"The police officer guarding Joe Owens's door asked me to give this to you." The guard handed over a piece of paper.

Martinez unfolded the sheet and read. He let out an audible sigh. "Thank goodness." He gave the paper to Ian.

Ian held the paper so Petra could also read what had been written. It was a short, simple note: "The doctor said that Joe Owens's vitals are improving. We expect him to regain consciousness by morning. He can be questioned by the police at that time."

"That's good news," said Petra. "Right?"

"That's great news," said Martinez.

Ian agreed. Because as soon as Joe Owens came out of his coma, he'd be able to tell the authorities what had happened—and hopefully clear Petra's name.

Chapter 8

Forty-five minutes. Such an insignificant amount of time, yet for Petra she felt every one of those lost minutes as a cut or a burn. If Joe woke up, she'd get all of the time back. Yet despite what she'd said, was Petra really ready for the truth? Was she prepared to face the fact that she might be an evil person?

"What's good news?" The question came from over Petra's shoulder and she turned to the voice. Rick Albright stood near the table. He wore his lab coat with his name embroidered over his breast pocket and a stethoscope looped over the back of his neck.

"Rick." Petra grew flustered. She wasn't sure why she should be—after all, Rick was the team doctor. He had a right to information about his star player.

"It's Joe," she said. She handed over the note that

had been delivered to Martinez. "It looks like he's going to recover."

"At least enough to tell us what happened," Martinez added. He got up from the table. "I have some phone calls to make."

"And will one of those be to your supervisor?" Ian asked. Petra knew what he expected the subject to be—the fact that Martinez never should've been involved in the case in the first place.

Martinez shook his head. "Let's see what Joe has to say when he wakes up."

Ian narrowed his eyes. "And then you'll say something—or I will."

"I appreciate all the time I can get." Before the cop was out of earshot, he was speaking on the phone. "There've been some developments," he said. Petra didn't hear the rest of the conversation; the smack of shoe leather on tile swallowed up Martinez's words. And then even his footfalls faded to nothing.

Rick dropped into the chair that the detective had just vacated. "What's happening with Joe?" he asked.

"You know as much as we do," said Ian. "Only what was in the note."

"Interesting," said Rick. He pushed Martinez's forgotten coffee cup to the middle of the table. "The last I heard was that he wasn't expected to make it."

"Joe's tough," said Petra. "I never doubted that he'd pull through."

"I'm not sure I agree," said Rick. "Considering…"

"Considering what?" Ian asked.

Rick scratched the side of his cheek. "I really shouldn't be discussing a patient of mine."

"If you have something to add," said Ian, "you should tell us now. Petra's life is on the line."

The doctor pivoted in his seat and looked at the door. He turned back and dropped his eyes to the table. "Joe had changed recently. You must've noticed, Petra."

She leaned back in the seat, her arms folded across her chest. She didn't like what Rick was suggesting, even if it cleared her name. "Joe was reacting to the divorce."

"It was before that. Why do you think his wife left?"

"Drugs?" asked Ian.

"If you mean illegal or recreational drugs, I doubt it. Guys who party too hard rarely last in professional sports."

"Performance enhancer?" suggested Ian.

"As long as the tests know what to look for, sure," said Rick.

Petra asked, "You think that Joe Owens was taking a performance enhancing drug that's so new, it's not something that can be caught on a standard test? Did Joe ever tell you that he was using experimental drugs?"

"No," said Rick. "Never. It just makes sense…"

"What about CTE?" asked Petra. "We've seen players who've suffered multiple concussions act in erratic ways."

"A chronic traumatic encephalopathy diagnosis

can't be made until after death," said Rick. He exhaled. "I'm on shaky professional ground, although I do want to help." He gave her a small smile.

"Thanks, Rick," she said. "You're a good friend."

"By the way," asked Ian, "who would have access to cutting-edge drugs like that?"

"I hate to say it, but I'm suspicious of the one person who benefits the most from Joe doing really well."

"Arnie Hatch," said Ian.

Rick looked over his shoulder again. "It's the only scenario that makes sense. Hatch has loads of money and can probably pay for his own research and development. Joe's a great player, but he wants to be a legend."

Petra slumped in her seat. Rick was right. Joe was driven, and drive that was left unchecked could quickly become unhealthy. "What do you think Hatch has to do with the attack?"

"Nothing," said Rick. "Or maybe everything. If Joe was on some kind of drug, he might have gone crazy. The wound could be self-inflicted. Or he could've had more trouble with other people—dangerous people—and no one would ever know—"

Ian interrupted, "Are these just guesses, or do you know something?"

Rick shook his head. "It's all conjecture on my part, but I don't think I'm wrong. And besides, if Joe's been taking untested drugs, we can't even guess how he'll react when he comes out of the coma."

Petra let the words sink in. She couldn't imagine

her client, usually so full of life and power, somehow extinguished.

"How are you feeling?" asked Rick, abruptly changing the subject. "Have you remembered anything at all?"

And there it was—the truth that perhaps she was responsible for extinguishing the light that was Joe Owens. Petra shook her head. "I can't recall a thing." She stopped. No, that wasn't true. "There was a scent. I can't quite describe it—sour, maybe."

"Good, good," said Rick. "The olfactory sense is the strongest. Anything else?"

"No," she said. "There's nothing."

Ian leaned forward. He met Petra's gaze, his gray eyes holding all the intensity of a thunderstorm. "What do you remember?"

"I recall being in Joe's house. I had a headache. I was almost blind with pain and felt like I was going to faint," said Petra.

"Think," urged Ian. "Those memories are close, I can tell."

Petra closed her eyes and brought back the the moment. "There was a noise behind me, like a shuffle."

"Anything else?" Ian asked.

Eyes still closed, she placed herself mentally in the hallway. "It was dark. There was a gurgling. And…"

"And what?" asked Rick.

The memory came to her with such clarity that the agony stole her breath. "There was a pain at the back of my head before I passed out."

She opened her eyes. Ian was staring at her. "A pain? Like you were hit from behind?"

Before Petra could answer, Rick was on his feet and standing at the back of her chair.

"Can I have a look?" He parted her hair, his fingertips gentle but cold.

"Sure," she said.

"Hmm," he murmured, gently probing her scalp. "You definitely have a contusion—a really big bruise. What I can't tell is how you got it. You might've been hit," he said. "Or you might have simply fainted and fallen backward, thus the bruise at the back of your head."

That wasn't right. She remembered the cold tile on her face as she blacked out. "I remember hitting my cheek on the floor," Petra said.

"Perhaps you pitched backward and hit a wall, or more likely a corner, and then fell forward. But it's good that you're remembering. I have a colleague who specializes in amnesia. I'll speak to her and give you a call." Rick stepped away from Petra. "I have a few things to check on before leaving the hospital, but I'll be in touch."

"Rick," she called out. "You don't have my new number." She handed him the cell phone Ian had lent her and waited while Rick copied down her new contact information.

He handed back the phone. "Thanks," he said and gave a little wave and then left the cafeteria.

Petra's bones hurt. Her eyes itched. She wanted to sleep and sleep and sleep. "What now?" she asked.

"I want to check Martinez's alibi."

"How are you going to do that?" Petra asked with a laugh. She added, "Hack into Gamblers Anonymous?"

Ian looked her in the eye and lifted one brow.

It was exactly what he planned to do.

Within a minute, he had managed to locate the check-in list for the GA meeting Luis had claimed to attend, using the RMJ software on his smartphone. The detective had been third on the list to sign in.

"It's not conclusive. I mean, someone might have signed in with his name. We still have to speak with a representative of the organization who can identify Martinez and verify that he attended the meeting," said Ian. "But for now, it corroborates his story nicely."

"Which means he had nothing to do with Joe's attack. And if we can't find anything new on Hatch, then there really isn't anyone left." She swallowed. "Besides me."

"I still don't like the connection to Yuri Kuzntov."

"The dead Russian."

"The way you say it makes him sound like a drink."

"With lots of vodka, I'm sure." She smiled, but it felt unfamiliar. Gritty with fear. She pressed her lips together.

Ian reached across the table and held her hand. "It'll be okay."

"I want to believe you," she said.

"Then do," he answered.

* * *

Ian didn't like Rick Albright, not at all. Then again, the team doctor had some interesting theories about what happened to Joe Owens.

He needed to find another suspect for the attack on Joe. The need to do so—for Petra's sake—filled him with determination. Maybe he had been too hasty when discarding Yuri. Maybe there was some information he'd overlooked on Joe's phone.

He scanned the cafeteria. At this time in the afternoon, it was almost completely empty. There was certainly enough privacy at the table to do a little sleuthing.

He opened a secure Rocky Mountain Justice app and remotely accessed the server. There was a new message. The information he'd gotten from the laptop at the raid had been opened. Ian's finger trembled as he pulled up the notice.

A single document had been accessed. It was an email from two months prior, sent to Yuri Kuzntov and written in Russian. *Otets saitsya na prospekete 1434 Zapaadnyy Arvada. Zhdite dal neyshikh.* Ian mentally translated it into English. *The sire is staying at 1434 West Arvada. Wait for further instructions.*

Just as Ian first suspected, the trio of Comrades had been waiting for Nikolai Mateev, who was commonly referred to as *otets*, or *sire*.

"I have something to check out," said Ian. "It'll be dangerous, so I'm going to take you back to my house."

"Does it have to do with my case?"

"Possibly," he admitted.

"Then don't treat me like a child. I can't be shut out of my own life."

Ian began to speak, a refusal on his lips. He wanted to protect her, to always keep her safe. Nikolai Mateev was a dangerous man—deadly, really. But Petra had a right to clear her own name, and besides, Ian wanted her with him. He stood and held out his hand. She reached for him. Her palm was soft and she smelled of lavender.

"Where are we going?" she asked as he pulled her to her feet.

Honestly, Ian didn't know. The email was two months old. Nikolai might very well have moved on. Or *otets* could refer to someone else entirely. "I have an address," he said. "It came from the dead Russian's computer. And if it's who I think it is, this could be extremely dangerous, Petra."

She lifted the forgotten cup of coffee on the table. "To success," she said.

Ian took the cup and discarded it in a trash can. "If we get lucky, then we'll have a proper toast of single malt Scotch. Or better yet, champagne."

"And if we don't get lucky?"

Ian just shook his head. The light banter was nice, but what they were about to do—where they were about to go—was no laughing matter. Petra was right to wonder what would happen if they didn't have luck on their side. And though he'd never share it with her, there were two possible unfortunate outcomes. The first was that they'd find nothing. And the second was that they'd end up dead.

Petra leaned forward and peered out the windshield. The late day sun shone down on the road and waves of heat undulated from the pavement. Before her was an apartment complex arranged in a horseshoe of three-story buildings, with a courtyard in the middle. She sat back in the seat. "Who are we looking for again?" she asked. In truth, he hadn't told her who he was after in the first place.

Ian gestured. "See that apartment? Third floor. Second one from the left."

Petra found the balcony. "Yeah."

"What do you think?" he asked. "Is anyone home?"

Behind the balcony was a sliding glass door. The curtains were opened and the room beyond was dark. "It looks empty to me," she said.

"That's just what I was thinking. The intel I got on this place is old—as in months old. I don't even know if the suspect is here."

"Suspect?" The word grabbed Petra's attention. "Do you think whoever's in there tried to kill Joe?"

Neck bent to look out the window, Ian shook his head. "Not exactly… But this might be the guy pulling all the strings. He'd know who attacked Joe and why."

"And let me guess—you want to know if it's safe to break in to that apartment."

"Exactly," said Ian. "But if someone is home, I might be recognized and shot on sight."

His words were glib and yet chilling. "I can go," she said. "I can knock on the door and see if anyone answers."

"No way," said Ian. "It's too dangerous."

"Let me do this, Ian. If it helps to find out what happened to Joe, then I want to. Besides, how much of a problem is it to knock on a door?"

"It's not the knocking that bothers me," said Ian. "It's who might answer."

"And who are you expecting?" she asked, suddenly afraid of what he might say.

"It's the associate of Yuri Kuzntov's. The man I knew from my days with MI5. His name is Nikolai Mateev and now he runs the world's largest criminal enterprise."

Nikolai Mateev. There was that name again. It was the same person Ian had been pursuing two years ago and the single most important person in Ian's life.

She never knew why and bit the inside of her lip to keep from saying more. There were more immediate problems than all the secrets Ian was willing to keep, especially if he was willing to talk now.

"And you think he tried to kill my client?" she asked.

"I don't know what to think. That's why I want to get into that apartment and look around."

"Then let me go."

Ian shook his head. "I'll figure something out, but I'm not asking you to put yourself in danger."

"I'm not looking for your permission, Ian. I'm

going." He began to speak, to argue. She held up her hand. "This is a job that needs to be done. If not, we may never know what happened to Joe."

"This isn't a game, Petra."

"I know. I've seen the dead Russian. I've also knelt next to my client while he bled out, with his blood all over my hands. I can't just walk away."

"I wasn't planning on walking away, just not using you as a decoy."

Petra quickly devised a plan. "I'll knock on the door. If someone answers, I'll ask for Tammy. If need be, I'll give them the apartment one flight down."

"No," said Ian.

"No? Why not?"

"First, those Russians are dangerous and smart. They'll see right through any ruse."

"And second?"

"Your safety is the only thing I care about."

Ian's words deserved to be examined. But not now. Now they had to get into that apartment—Petra's life depended on it.

"If you can't go, and I can't go—call someone else."

"Like who?"

"Call Roman," she said.

"Mateev knows Roman."

"What about Julia?"

"So she can ask if Tammy's home, too?"

"Do you have a better plan?"

Ian leaned back into the seat and rubbed his forehead. "We wait. We watch. We see if anyone shows up."

"And if they don't?"

"Then I'm going in and I'll lay a trap for those bastards."

Ian used a set of high-powered binoculars that he kept stowed in the SUV to watch the apartment. It had been two hours since they arrived, and nothing had changed.

After years of working in the field, Ian knew there was no such thing as surety, but he was fairly certain that there was no one at home. Had it been abandoned? Or was it simply that the occupants were away?

"I'm going up there," he said, handing Petra the binoculars. "You stay here. If I'm not back in five minutes, call the police."

"Ian," said Petra, her voice breathless. "Don't leave me." Despite the air-conditioning, a bead of sweat dotted her upper lip. She wiped it away. "I don't know how to explain it, but I don't want to be left alone."

It was residual terror from blacking out and finding her injured client, he knew. A fear that if left alone, she wouldn't be able to control herself. Sure, taking her with him might slow down Ian's search of the apartment, yet he couldn't leave her in the car to have a full-blown panic attack.

"Come with me," he said before he could change his mind.

They quickly crossed the street and climbed to the third-floor landing.

Ian pressed his lips to Petra's ear. "Wait here. If

you hear anything, and I mean anything, walk away. Call the police but keep going. Promise me."

"I promise," she whispered back, her breath washing over his neck.

Ian's body reacted with memories of her passionate whispers. He refocused his attention and turned for the apartment. A railing ran the length of the walkway, but Ian kept close to the building to decrease his profile. He stopped at the door. Tarnished brass numbers were affixed to the wall: 346.

He knocked. There was nothing. He knocked again. Still no answer. After withdrawing a file from his jeans pocket, he jimmied the lock, and within a second, the door swung open.

Ian stepped into the small apartment and the scent hit him full in the face. Trash mixed with body odor, and underneath it all was something more—sweet and rotten. Decay?

Carpet, which might have begun as any color but was now gray with filth, covered the floor. The apartment was a single room. Living area, kitchen, a hospital bed. A bathroom was tucked into a corner. Litter was strewn everywhere. Newspapers were piled on the floor in teetering stacks. Dirty dishes sat on the counter. Half-filled beer bottles stood sentry in the corners.

Was this where Nikolai Mateev lived? Truly, Ian had a hard time imagining such a powerful man residing in this dump of a flat. At the same time, it was a brilliant way to avoid detection—just like when

Mateev took a Greyhound bus into the country from British Columbia.

"Ian?" Petra stood on the threshold. She watched him, her brows drawn together. "I couldn't just stay on the landing. I know what you said. I'm sorry."

He held up his hands, traffic-cop style. "Wait there," he said. "I don't want you to come inside."

"Why not?"

It was a reasonable question. And yet this place was tainted of Mateev. Ian didn't want any of it to touch Petra.

"I need two minutes, Petra. You'd be safest in the car." He doubted that she'd agree.

"Just do your search. I'll be fine, I promise."

Ian turned from her and picked up a newspaper. It was a copy of the *Novaya Gazeta* dated two weeks ago. Goose bumps broke out on Ian's skin.

He knelt next to the pile of papers and began to shuffle through the copies. They were Russian, all of them. *The Commersant. Informpolis.* There were even copies of the Red Army's official newspaper, *Krasnaya Zvezda.* But the most recent one was from last week. Was it because no one lived here anymore or because Russian papers weren't readily available in Denver?

Ian stood and searched the table. There, under a ketchup-stained napkin, was a yellow-gold prescription bottle. And another and another. On the end table there were two more. He jerked the covers from the bed. Three more pill bottles rolled across the floor.

Ian picked one up and read the name: John Smith.

Another prescription was made out to David Carpenter. A third to Robert Edgars. Ian didn't believe that there were several sick people living here—all with Anglo-sounding names and who just so happened to read Russian papers. It was one person, with enough influence and cash to get prescriptions under several different aliases.

It was Mateev. It had to be. Now Ian needed to figure out how to turn Mateev's lair into his coffin.

Nikolai sat in the back of the car. The latest doctor's appointment had proved to be more painful than he'd anticipated. He longed for relief from the unending fatigue and relentless pain.

And yet…he knew the prognosis. Knew the likely outcome. Did he have the strength, under these conditions, to continue this fight?

Head slumped against the tinted window, he watched his reflection superimposed on the passing traffic. Fast-food restaurants. Used car lots. Strip malls with frozen yogurt stands and laundromats. His eyes hurt and his head pounded. He leaned back in the seat and pinched the bridge of his nose. The twang of a country song blared from the speakers.

"Pickup trucks and beer. That isn't music, just noise. Turn that crap off," he ordered. "I can't listen anymore."

"You need anything else?" Ilya asked, silencing the music. "Something to eat? It's lunchtime."

"There is nothing for me in America," Nikolai said. "It's a wonder this country became a superpower at all. They are stupid and lazy. They take offense at everything and are easily distracted by the next vice."

"But that makes them good customers," said Anatoly.

Nikolai gave a quiet laugh.

"Drugs. Booze. Prostitutes," he said. "Their weaknesses have made me a rich man."

"Do you want to go home?" Anatoly asked.

He didn't mean to the nasty apartment they'd all been sharing for the past two months, but rather to Russia. At home, Nikolai was treated like a king. In America? He was forced to hide, like vermin in the sewer. The only time he left his hiding place was to see more doctors. For in America, they also had the best medical care.

"I can't go back," he muttered. "I need to be here for my appointments, at least for now."

Pancreatic cancer. It was a quick death sentence to most, but Nikolai had refused to succumb to his illness, and had survived for more than three years as a sick man. The treatments found in the Russian Federation—the chemotherapy and radiation—had left him weaker than the actual illness.

And then he'd heard of a miracle and came to America. It had been developed without any oversight from the government and was only available to people wealthy enough and desperate enough to pay.

It was perfect for Nikolai Mateev.

Yet only in America.

America. The word made him gag.

The sun beat down on the car, the interior so stifling that Nikolai couldn't draw a breath. "Turn up the air conditioner, will you? I'm about to suffocate."

"Sure thing," said Anatoly. He moved his hand to the controls, but stopped when he realized the air was already on full.

Sweat dampened Nikolai's hair and dripped down his back. He was going crazy. Hiding and waiting and watching had finally driven him mad. "Stop here," he said. "I'll walk."

The car pulled up to the next corner and he stumbled out. The front passenger door also opened. Ilya placed one foot on the sidewalk, ready to accompany the boss. Nikolai held up a hand. "Don't. I'll walk."

The bodyguard hesitated. "I should stay with you. It's not safe."

Nikolai stood straight, still impressive despite everything. "There's no danger," he sighed. "No one even knows who I am in this dump. Go and get a pizza or something. We should've had dinner hours ago."

The door closed and the sedan merged into traffic. Within a minute the car was gone and he was alone. His loathsome apartment was just across the street, and yet it might as well have been a hundred kilometers through a minefield.

When did he become a child, frightened by…well, anything?

The walk would do him good, he decided. He took one step and then another. His bones ached. He felt the rot inside him. But with each step, some of the pain left. He felt the warmth of the sun kiss his face. He would not be defeated so easily by the poison in his body.

Nikolai strode through the courtyard. He looked up to his apartment and stopped short. A woman leaned on the railing. Even from three flights below, he could see that his door was ajar. His heart raced as he stood there, immobile with indecision.

Think, damn it.

He knew one thing: she wasn't with the police. They would have brought a battalion of men, with cars and guns. Snipers would've been placed on the rooftops. Nikolai instinctively stepped under an eave and looked up. There were no black helmets, no tell-tale flash of a scope reflecting the sunshine. Everything was as it should be—except for the woman.

Who was she? Was she alone? And what if she wasn't? He wondered, briefly, whether an agent from Rocky Mountain Justice could have caught his trail… that, at least, would have made sense to him. A single actor, or two, refusing to follow the rule of law. It was easier for them to seek him out. They weren't bound by the legalities of the American agencies.

He sank deeper into the shadows. Prudence told him he should leave and contact his bodyguards. They were only going to get pizza and could be here in less than five minutes and then Nikolai would disappear. But then what would that mean? Had he truly become ancient and infirmed, chased away by a girl?

He watched her from the shadows, a predator with its prey. The woman checked her phone and gave a disgruntled sigh. Even from the ground, he could see the firm set of her jaw and the furrow between her eyebrows. He was adept at reading people and without question, this woman was waiting, and unhappy. It also meant she was far from vigilant.

A plan came quickly. It was simple and brutal, and best of all, required no one but himself.

Walking quietly up the stairs, he paused on the landing. His breathing was labored and the pain in his bones had returned. Yet his pulse was strong and power flowed through his veins. He braced his legs and charged. The woman looked up and gasped at the sight of him. Eyes wide, her jaw hung open. Nikolai Mateev shoved the woman and she tumbled over the railing.

Chapter 9

Ian heard Petra's scream, and his blood turned cold. He leaped from the floor and sprinted out the door.

The walkway was empty. Petra was gone—vanished. The echo of her shriek had already faded.

He turned in a quick circle, his eyes taking in everything at once. He saw them—a set of hands, clutching the bottom rung of the railing. Petra. Her knuckles were white.

He dived forward and grasped her wrists. "I've got you," he said. "But don't let go."

Petra stared up at him. Her face was chalky and her skin was damp with perspiration. His hands slid. He clasped tighter, his fingers biting into her arm. She squirmed and her feet thrashed. One shoe slipped from her foot, silently somersaulting through the air before landing with a thump in the courtyard below.

"Ian," she gasped. Her own hands slid, until just her fingers were hooked over the metal rung. "I can't hold on much longer."

A sharp crack broke the afternoon quiet. It registered as a gunshot and Ian flattened completely.

Just as quickly, he realized that the noise hadn't come from a firearm, but someplace just as deadly. One of three bolts that held the section of railing in place had cracked. The entire structure bowed outward. Petra screamed, but didn't let go.

If one of the other bolts broke, the whole section would topple, sending Petra to the courtyard twenty feet below. Then again, maybe that was the best way to save her life.

"Look at me," Ian said to her. She lifted her wide eyes to his. "I have an idea. It's a longshot, but the only shot I have."

Her face went gray. "Okay," she said. "I trust you."

"I'm going to let go of your arms," he said.

Petra began to shake her head. "No, Ian. Don't. This railing's weak. It could fall at any minute."

He ignored the fear in her voice and the dread in her expression. "That's what I'm counting on. I'm going to kick the other bolts loose."

"You're going to what?"

"You have to hold on to the railing and I'll lower it down. At the end, you'll have to drop, but it'll only be a few feet."

"What if you can't hold on to the railing?"

That was the real question, wasn't it? Ian refused to fail. The alternative would be devastating to Petra—to him. "I won't let you get hurt," he vowed.

Petra bit her bottom lip. Their eyes met. "There's no other way, is there?"

Ian shook his head. "Hold on," he warned, "and don't let go until I tell you."

"Got it," she said.

Ian paused, his hands on her wrists. He wanted to tell her more, say something. But what? The moment was too important to waste on words.

"Don't let go," he said again.

He stood and aimed his toe at the middle bolt. He kicked. His foot connected with solid metal. He kicked again and again. The railing undulated.

"Ian," Petra said, fear in her voice, "I can't hold on."

The bolt cracked and the whole railing flipped outward. Petra bounced, jostled like a rag doll. But her grip held. Ian grabbed the fastened end of the railing and shoved, once, twice, feeling his muscles burn with the effort. The final bolt broke. The whole segment teetered and Ian braced his legs. The weight of the railing, plus Petra's slim body, pulled him forward.

His arms ached. Sweat streamed into his eyes, blinding him. He took one step, until the tips of his shoes were even with the edge of the walkway, and glanced down. Petra dangled from the segment of railing, still several feet from the ground.

"I can't lower you any more," he said. "You'll have to jump."

Petra looked over her shoulder and then back at him. She closed her eyes and let go.

Petra hit the ground, feet, knees, face. For a moment, she was back in Joe Owens's hallway. Her head was pounding. There was shuffling from behind and then pain exploded at the back of her skull. She tried to grasp the memory, but it slipped away, like sand through her fingers.

The metal railing clattered to the ground behind her. She stood, and pain shot through her ankle. She hobbled forward and looked up. Ian remained on the third floor. The sun shone down, surrounding him in a halo. He really was her guardian angel.

"Are you okay?" he called.

"I'm standing," she said, "which means a lot."

"Stay where you are. I'm coming to you."

Ian was at her side in an instant. He wrapped his arms around her waist and pulled her to him. Petra leaned into the embrace, allowing him to keep her upright.

"You're safe," he said. He stroked back her hair. "How did you end up out there? Did you fall? Faint?"

Petra shook her head. "It all happened so quickly, but there was a man. He came out of nowhere, rushed at me and pushed me over the railing. Thank God I was able to grab it as I fell." She melted into Ian's chest. His strength and warmth made her feel safe and alive.

He went rigid. "A man? What man?"

"It's not someone I know, if that's what you're asking."

"Did he say anything? Could you tell if he had an accent?"

Petra backed away. "What are you thinking? That I was attacked by some Russian drug lord?"

"I don't know what to think. But we should get out of here, in case the guy comes back. Can you walk?" Ian retrieved her lost shoe. "Should I take you to the hospital?"

Petra slipped the ballet flat on, then winced as she put pressure on her foot. But it wasn't a stabbing pain that made her think she'd broken anything vital. "Honestly, I'm fine. Sore, but fine."

Ian wrapped his arm around her once more, taking much of her weight. He led her through the courtyard and back to the road. "Did you see the man's face? Would you recognize him if you saw him again?"

"Maybe," said Petra. "He was an older guy. Caucasian. White hair. He was big and obviously strong. Sound like someone you know?"

"Could be. Let's get you into the car." Ian helped Petra across the street and held her steady as she climbed into the SUV. He rounded to the other side and got into the driver's seat. After pulling the door closed, he asked, "Would you be willing to look at a picture?"

Petra didn't have the energy to fight. "Sure," she said.

Ian took a tablet computer from the glove compartment and tapped on the screen. He handed the device to Petra. She stared at a black-and-white image of three men standing next to a large sedan. Collars on trench coats were pulled high. One man held a cigarette. A haze of smoke surrounded his head.

"Is the man who attacked you in this picture? Keep in mind, this photo was taken more than ten years ago, so he might've aged since."

Petra handed the computer back to Ian. "I don't recognize any of them."

"Are you sure?"

She closed her eyes, bringing back the split second when the man had attacked. Her heart raced and her stomach reeled with the weightlessness. The man's face had been red and covered with a sheen of sweat. His eyes were narrowed. His mouth was twisted in a sneer.

She opened her eyes and looked at the photo again. The man with the cigarette had his lip lifted in a sneer. She pointed to the picture. "It might be him."

"Are you sure?" asked Ian.

"Not really," said Petra, with a shake of her head. She looked at the picture again. All three men had similar builds, similar looks. "It could be any of them, or none of them. I'm sorry I'm not more helpful. We should still call the police. There's a madman on the loose and we don't want him to hurt anyone else."

"No," said Ian.

Petra's hand trembled with pent-up frustration. "No? No? Why not?"

"For starters, we knew where he was, not where

he is. If it is Nikolai, he won't come back to this apartment, if for no other reason than his safe house has been made. He's not that stupid."

"Then call the police so they can look for him."

"Sure, but for what? An old guy with white hair and a bad attitude?"

She tried to think of something to say. But why? Ian would counter any argument she made—he always did. "I can't believe you won't call."

"I don't need the police, because I'm going to handle Nikolai Mateev my way."

Her breath stilled, as if her body understood his meaning a split second before her brain. "This is why you shut down RMJ, this is the secret you won't share with me. You don't want anyone else involved because you're going after him yourself. I'm right, aren't I?"

Ian leaned his arm on the door handle. Thumbnail pressed to his lip, he looked out the window. He didn't deny her accusation. He didn't respond to her question. And that was an answer all on its own.

"Who is he?"

"Nikolai Mateev. I've told you that already."

"You can't be that cold-blooded, Ian." He still gazed out the window. Petra tried to guess what had captured his attention. She saw nothing beyond his reflection, faint and distorted.

"I should've killed Mateev years ago."

"Damn it, Ian, you aren't so unfeeling as to murder someone, if that's what you plan to do. How can you not care about what's right and wrong?"

"I quit having feelings a long time ago. And there's nothing I won't do to stop Mateev—lie, cheat, kill."

Then she understood something else, as well. "You aren't really helping me, either, are you? Joe knew your dead Russian, who knew Mateev. And you think that by finding Joe's attacker, you'll find Nikolai."

"It's not that I'm not helping you," said Ian. "But we can have different needs that meet the same goal."

Different needs. That had been their problem all along. How had she not seen it then? Like a good mystery, the clues had all been there; she'd just refused to look.

No longer. From here on out, Petra knew what she was dealing with—a man who was ruled by his obsessions. Despite the pain in her chest, she laughed out loud. The sound was hollow.

"So now this is all amusing?"

Wiping her eyes, she said, "It's not funny at all. Sad, more like it. Ever since I showed up at your house, I've had this fantasy that…I don't know, things might work out between us. That somehow I wasn't responsible for Joe being in the hospital, and in the end, you and I would be happy and together."

"And that's sad?"

"It is if it'll never happen. And it won't, Ian. Even if you found Nikolai Mateev and killed him today, it'd never happen. You know why?"

"No," he grumbled, "but I assume that you're going to tell me."

"Because you will always be consumed with something, but it will never be me. I'm not the thing that will keep you awake at night or working until dawn."

Turning his gaze to the window, he said, "That's not fair. Everything I did, I did for you—for us."

She wanted to laugh again, or maybe just cry. "Do you really believe that, Ian? Or was it all an excuse—just like helping me with Joe got you close to Mateev?"

He turned to her, and his look had the power of a hurricane. He could storm all he wanted. This time, she refused to back down. "I can't help you murder an innocent man."

"Nikolai Mateev is a lot of things. Innocent isn't one of them."

"See?" she said. "That's it exactly. I can't compete with your fixations. Nothing can."

"What do you want me to say? I told you the truth. I am helping you, but I'm also helping myself. There's no rule that says I can't get something I need, too." He looked back to the window and gave a snort of a laugh. "Or is there? Is there some unwritten rule you have where I should focus only on you?"

As if she'd gotten sucker punched, her middle contracted and she felt as if she might retch. And yet she had been struck—with the force of his words. "We aren't going anywhere else. Take me home, Ian."

"What about the media? I thought they were camped out at your complex."

"I just need to get away," she said. The words felt heavy on her tongue.

"That's your answer to everything, isn't it, Petra?"

He started the engine and pulled onto the street. "Whenever anything gets too hard, you run away."

"Knowing that I'll never be important enough for you, and then leaving, isn't running away. It's being smart."

"That's the thing with me, though, Petra. I don't quit. I don't leave because things get tough. I might not have been home for dinner every night, but I always came home. I never left—not even after you were gone."

Thank goodness the TV reporters had tired of waiting for Petra and had left the complex. The air in her apartment was stale and pressed down on her flesh. She shut the door and dropped her purse on the coffee table. The bag fell to the side and her eye was drawn to Ian's. Damn. She'd have to see him one more time to return his cell and get her car.

Or better yet, she'd take an Uber to his house, then mail the damn phone, along with a note that he should donate her clothes to a worthy organization.

With that decision made, she dropped to the sofa and let her body meld into the cushions. Her life was far from perfect. Accused of attempted murder, no job, no money—and now, no Ian. But she'd walked away from harsh circumstances before and survived. She assumed that she could do it again.

It's just that she'd gotten used to having Ian at her side again, which was clearly a huge mistake.

Petra inhaled deeply, hoping that a few yoga breaths would settle her nerves...but something unfamiliar sent a bolt of fear through her. She sat up, her spine rigid, her heart racing. The smell…what was it? It was like spoiled milk. Had something gone bad in just two days? And why was it so frightening? Or maybe residual emotions from all she had gone through would put her on edge from now on.

Petra wandered to the kitchen and opened the fridge. A swath of yellow light illuminated a wedge of the floor. The nearly empty shelves held salad fixings and a bag of deli meat. Nothing out of the ordinary. And yet…

She looked over her shoulder into the living room. The last rays of sun were retreating across the space as the day ended. She looked up at the TV mounted to the wall. The room was reflected in the screen, but she swore that she saw…something. A shadow… a man.

No. Just her imagination.

She turned on a lamp, the artificial light spilling across the floor. Then she moved to the blinds and pulled them closed, safely hiding her away. Tension she didn't recall holding slipped from her shoulders and she exhaled.

"Maybe if I ate," she said out loud, if for no other reason than she needed to hear the sound of a human voice. She grabbed a bundle of kale from the fridge and began to rinse it at the sink. The sound of a footfall came from behind.

Petra whirled around. There was no one.

She turned back to the counter and grabbed a knife from the block. She glanced once more over her shoulder before stripping the leaves from the stalks. The juices stained her hands and the scent of freshly cut greens filled the kitchen, overpowering the lingering stink of rot.

The lights went out.

She froze.

A fist connected with her spine. Petra lurched forward. Pain shot through her body. She could not breathe, could not move, could not think.

A hand grabbed the back of her hair, slamming her face into the counter. The coppery taste of blood filled her mouth as her lips began to throb. By instinct alone, she pushed off the counter with all her weight, knocking her attacker off balance.

Her head snapped back. Her attacker's hand was still tangled in her hair. The force sent them both to the kitchen floor. They landed on their backs, with her atop him. Like she had so many times on the basketball court, Petra drove her elbow into his stomach. He wheezed with the impact and the grip on her hair released.

She scrambled to her feet, lunging for the door. A hand wrapped around her foot and yanked up. Petra tumbled forward, hitting the floor hard. She flipped onto her back and kicked out as a form grew from the darkness, connecting with the man's middle. With a muttered curse, he stumbled back.

On hands and knees, she crawled forward. The door was so near, if she just reached out she could touch the handle.

Another blow struck her on the side of the head.

Petra's ears buzzed. Tears filled her eyes. She fell to the side, her shoulder hitting the coffee table. The lamp tumbled to the ground.

Then he was upon her. Pinning her to the ground, burying her face in the carpeting—smothering her, forcing her hot breath back into her lungs. His hands moved to her throat, his fingers dug into her neck and her breathing stopped. She bucked and writhed, anything to get him off her, to force him to let go. His grip tightened and her vision started to fade. Her arms grew heavy and limp. She dropped her hands away and her fingertips brushed something solid and metal.

For a moment, she didn't care. Then she realized what she touched. The lamp. A crude weapon, but something she could use to strike her attacker nonetheless. She reached for the base and wrenched her arm back. She heard the satisfying crack of metal on bone as the light connected with her assailant.

He pulled his hands away with a howl of pain, and sweet, clean air rushed into Petra's lungs. She tried to crawl forward, but he still sat on her back, pinning her to the floor. With both hands, her attacker pushed her into the carpet again. She swung the lamp back, striking him again and again. He gripped the base, pulling it from her grasp. But his weight shifted, and she squirmed free.

On her feet, she rushed not for the door, but the kitchen. Her ears buzzed. Her throat burned. Her vision was filled with a thousand bursting stars. Yet there was only one way she'd make it out of her condo alive. Petra grabbed the knife she'd used for the kale.

The man, just a shadow in the darkness, rushed toward her.

Without thought, she lunged, gripping the hilt of her knife in both hands.

Chapter 10

Ian stared at the entrance to Petra's condominium complex. The wrought iron gate wound around at the top, the filigree reminding him of the fences near St. James's Park. Maybe going back to England was the answer. In truth, without Mateev, or RMJ, or Petra, there was nothing in the States for him.

She deserved better than him, a man whose sense of justice was so keen that he'd willingly sacrifice everything—even her—to serve the greater good.

Like a snake eating its tail, it brought him back to his original question. How were Joe Owens and Nikolai Mateev connected? Beyond Yuri, the dead Russian, there was nothing to directly link the two. But if Nikolai wasn't involved in Joe's attack, then who was? Tighter and tighter the coils wound, and Ian felt the squeezing in his chest.

Well, he'd do no good sitting here. After putting the gearshift into Reverse, Ian backed out of the parking space. He turned the wheel and maneuvered onto the street. He glanced out the window one last time.

She was there. Petra. Her hair streamed behind her. Even in the dark, he could tell that her face was bloodied. Blood covered her clothes. Ian's heart stopped for a single beat, seized with terror that he might actually lose Petra. Then his blood began to flow again, hot and full of fury that he'd once again failed to protect her. He threw the vehicle into Park and sprinted to her side.

"What happened?" he said, pulling her into his arms. She was shaking and he held her tighter.

"There was someone in my apartment. He attacked me, but I got away."

Ian's spine stiffened. "Did he hurt you? You're bleeding."

She touched her lip. "A little battered and bruised, but I'm okay."

Okay? She was far from okay. "You're covered in blood…"

"I stabbed the guy with a kitchen knife and just ran."

"Did you kill him?"

She shuddered in his arms. "I don't think so."

"But he might still be in your apartment."

"I guess," she said shakily. "I didn't stay around to see what he planned to do next."

"Did you see his face? Can you identify the attacker?"

"It was dark," she said. "He tried to choke me..." Petra's voice trailed off and he tried to think of something soothing to say. Nothing came to mind. He wasn't good with sharing his emotions.

"Get in the car," he said, "and lock the doors."

"If you think that I'm going to sit out here and wait for you while you check my apartment, you are crazy."

Ian didn't have time to argue. He wanted to get into her apartment. And if a neighbor heard or saw something? The police could be here in minutes and he didn't want deal with the cops. "Let's go," he said.

He'd never been to Petra's new condo, so she led him to her unit and stopped at the door. He pushed it open.

The only light in the dark room came from outside, illuminating a small section of carpeting. He found a light switch on the wall and turned it on. An overhead light illuminated the whole scene.

A trail of blood led from the kitchen to the door, where the knife lay in a puddle of red-black blood. A broken lamp lay in the middle of the room.

"He was stabbed near the kitchen," said Ian, putting together the story the evidence told him. "And dropped the lamp. Then he staggered to the door, where he pulled the knife free before leaving through the front door."

"Which means he's gone," said Petra.

"Most likely. Did he say anything? Was it the same

man from the apartment building? The one who threw you over the railing?"

"It wasn't him, for sure," she said with a shake of her head. "This guy was definitely younger. I could tell by his movements. Whoever it was must've been hiding in the bedroom or the bathroom, waiting for me. Do you think it was the same person who attacked Joe?"

Ian did, and she read the answer on his expression.

She folded her arms over her chest and looked around the room. "I'm not sure I can stay here tonight," she said, "or ever again."

"You can sleep at my place. But you should change before you leave and maybe even pack a bag for a few days."

"A few days?"

"Until we figure out who broke in to your home and attacked Joe, I'm not letting you leave my sight."

Ian had stood guard while Petra changed out of her soiled clothes and donned a khaki T-shirt dress and denim jacket. She filled a bag with more clothes and shoes and then they left for Ian's, since that was the only place he felt safe taking her.

It was almost ten o'clock by the time they pulled in to his circular driveway. While he prepared a quick dinner of pasta and salad, Petra sat in the living room and flipped from newscast to newscast. They were all the same. The attack on Joe Owens and Petra's alleged involvement was the top story.

She had a right to know what the media was saying about her—and yet, Ian couldn't help but think that there was a great deal of truth in the old adage that ignorance was bliss.

He filled two wineglasses and walked to the living room. Light from the TV bathed her in a silver light, and his pulse quickened at the sight of her.

She looked up as he approached. "Here," he said. "This will help calm your nerves."

Petra took the wine and sipped. "If anything else happens today, I'll need something stronger than this."

He laughed at her dark humor. "I wish the news was better, Petra, that they'd be reporting on how we caught the real culprit already."

"What if they have, Ian. What if it's me?"

He shook his head. "I refuse to believe that you're guilty."

"Well, that makes one."

"Sarcasm isn't going to solve this case," said Ian.

"What will, Ian? We've run down every reasonable lead to the attack. Face it, none of the other suspects had the opportunity or motive I did." She quietly cursed. "I'm going to spend my life in jail."

"There's the Yuri Kuzntov angle. Your client was buying drugs from some pretty dangerous men. And then there's the fact that someone attacked you in your own apartment."

"Which was more likely a deranged fan than a Russian gangster. The coverage has been nonstop. Half of Denver must want me dead."

"This conversation is getting us nowhere. Come

on," he said, holding out his hand. "Let's get some food. You'll feel better after you get something to eat."

She ignored his hand and stood. Wine sloshed over the rim of her glass. She bent to lick the liquid from her wrist. Just a flash of pink against her tanned skin. It was too much, and Ian's mind was filled with scenes of their lovemaking. He had to focus if he was going to help Petra, help himself, and he turned for the kitchen.

Ian had set the island in the kitchen with the basics. Plates. Utensils. Food. More wine.

While they both needed to eat, there was more that Ian wanted to discuss. He owed Petra an explanation. He owed her the truth.

"When I was a kid in England, I didn't have any goals for my life, didn't even plan to go to university. But a neighbor of mine, Travis Wetherby, had gone to Cambridge. Travis came home now and again to visit his mum, who lived down the way. Wetherby encouraged my studies and told me if I got the marks to get in, he'd pay my way at university."

"That was very generous of him," said Petra.

Ian nodded and took a drink of his wine. He let the liquid slide to his stomach and begin to warm him from within. "It was all the encouragement I needed and turned myself around. My marks improved, and I was accepted at Cambridge. Wetherby was true to his word and paid my way. About a month before graduation, Wetherby introduced me to his boss."

"And they were MI5," said Petra, guessing the next

part of his story. "You never told me how you got into the agency. I always assumed it was confidential."

"It is," said Ian with a shrug. "But I owe everything I am to Wetherby. Without him, I'd be in Manchester and turning old before my time."

Ian took several bites of pasta, giving himself time to think. He wasn't sure what he planned to share with Petra and what he needed to keep locked up in his memories.

"You were telling me about how you got your job with MI5," said Petra.

"It's not just about getting the job," he said.

She pinned him with her dark brown eyes, eyes where Ian could lose himself—if he weren't careful. "What's it about, then?"

"Sacrifice and honor and keeping promises... I need you to understand." Ian leaned forward and lowered his voice. "I need you to know why I have to kill Nikolai Mateev."

She sat back, her arms folded in that protective gesture she used all too often. Ian felt a seed of irritation grow as she protested, "You don't have to kill anyone—"

"Fifteen years ago," he began, cutting her off. "A lifetime, really, I was on my first assignment. I was in London—in Piccadilly Circus, in fact."

Ian tried to stay present, but that foggy London night returned to him and the damp air once again clung to his skin. The stones underfoot were slick with the recent rain; light reflected and wavered in the puddles.

"I saw him as I ran," he said. "At first he was just a figure in the distance, but I knew." Ian stopped and looked at his hands. "He was slumped against a corner and I turned him over. When I did, his coat slipped open and I saw his shirt. It was shredded from too many stab wounds and saturated with blood. It was him, Petra. It was Travis Wetherby."

"Oh, Ian," she said. She reached across the table and took his hand. He hardly felt the touch, his mind was so far into the past.

"What happened," he'd asked. His pulse raced and a stitch pulled at his side.

Travis had said, "I've been stabbed and that bloody Russian bastard got away. He has it in a leather case."

It. A dirty bomb.

Ian lifted his gaze to the empty square. Yet he had to get his supervisor help. The man was his friend, not just his recruiter. He withdrew his cell phone and hit the power button. The small wheel that indicated a search for a signal turned and turned. He cursed.

He felt Travis's cold hand on his. "Don't bother with me, lad. You have to stop the bloody bastard. He went to the Tube."

"I gave Travis my phone so he could at least call and get help for himself, but I did what he said. I left to go after the Russian and the bomb.

"I didn't want to leave him on the street, Petra. Travis Wetherby had given my life a purpose, but he would've been disappointed if I didn't do my duty." Ian took a swallow of his wine. The candlelight flickered before him, yet he saw the overhead fluorescent lights of the Tube station. The tracks slithered from one yawning tunnel to the next. The scents of motor oil and rubbish mingled in the air. Two homeless men, wrapped in dirty and rumpled trench coats, slept on a bench that was twenty yards farther up the platform.

"I knew that in a little more than sixty minutes the station would begin to fill with early morning commuters. And in less than three hours, more than one hundred thousand souls would pass that exact spot. Yet there was only one soul that concerned me—Nikolai Mateev, and he was gone.

"Like Travis taught me, I took in the whole scene, looking for that slight irregularity. The lights. The platform. The homeless men. And then I saw it. The trench coat lining on one man wasn't right. It was a bright red-and-black check."

"Burberry," Petra offered.

Ian gave a small laugh. "It was. The overhead light reflected off his very well polished shoes, too. And those were resting on a leather briefcase. I took a step toward them, just as the air started to hum with an oncoming train.

"Nikolai Mateev sprang to his feet, dragging the real homeless man up with him. He rushed toward the edge of the platform and pushed. With a single shriek, the poor fellow flew onto the tracks. The train rocketed closer to the platform and the homeless man scrambled to his feet. Mateev began to run toward the opposite exit."

Ian hesitated. "The question I asked myself then, as I do now, was should I save one person now or thousands later? I chose thousands. I ran after Mateev and tackled him round the middle. We tumbled to the ground and the case skidded from his grasp. There was a tussle, and in the end, Mateev let go. I reached for him—my fingers brushed the fabric of his belt.

"I remember the platform vibrating as the train came closer. Screams echoed off the walls—from the homeless man or the locomotive, I couldn't decide. In the end, I couldn't let one person die when I had the power to save him. I ran to the homeless man and reached for his hand, dragged him toward me. We landed on the concrete, a nuclear bomb between us."

"Then you're a hero, Ian. You saved one person and thousands."

He shook his head. "That's where you're wrong. I kept a bomb from exploding somewhere in London, but Nikolai Mateev has killed hundreds of thousands of people with his drugs alone. I let a monster go free. I cannot allow that failure to remain on my conscience."

"What happened to Travis?" Petra asked. It wasn't what he expected; he thought she'd tell him that all life was sacred. Then again, Travis was as much a part of this story as Ian or Mateev.

"A dozen uniformed bobbies descended the stairs as I was helping the homeless man to his feet. When I told them what had happened and that we needed to search the city for Mateev, they were astounded. One of them bet I'd get the MBE from the Queen, even.

"I remember thinking—a knight? Sir Ian Wallace? What a laugh. And I said something like, 'Wait until old Travis hears that one.' And then I thought to ask, 'How's my partner?

"The bobby told me that Travis had called in the whole thing. But when his gaze drifted to the floor, I knew. He didn't need to say more. Travis Wetherby was gone, and a part of me died that night."

Even now, Ian's throat itched and his eyes burned. He worked his jaw back and forth, until the pain left his chest. "Sure, we had the bomb—but Nikolai Mateev had gotten away. Travis gave his life for nothing.

"I left the Tube station and it had started to rain. I remember standing there, my face to the sky, mourning a man who had paid the ultimate price."

"Why now?" asked Petra. "Why go after Mateev now, and in Denver, no less?"

"The name Mateev surfaced last Christmas when Nikolai's daughter-in-law was accused of kidnapping her own son and bringing him from New York to Colorado. I knew then that fate had given me a second chance to keep the most important promise I ever made—to avenge Travis Wetherby's death."

Nikolai sat on the bed in his newest safe house. This was, by far, the worst place he'd stayed. A single bulb hung from the ceiling, casting a sickly yellow pool on the floor. To him, it looked like a puddle of urine on the concrete. The scent of motor oil was heavy in the air and coated his lips.

He'd been moved to a cavernous dark warehouse. Beyond the pool of piss-colored light, oil drums were stacked one atop the other, soaring to the ceiling. In the half-light they looked like the cooling towers of Chernobyl.

He still remembered the ground shaking underfoot and the blast of hot air as the explosion reached him twenty kilometers away. The doctors in Kiev had told him there was nothing in the nuclear blast to concern him. And good foolish communist that he was, Nikolai had believed them.

Then his wife had a baby, a sickly girl with only one lung and a cleft palate. The child died within days and the doctors in Moscow told him it was bad luck and had nothing to do with his time in the Ukraine.

But by then Nikolai knew better. He had a son living in America who was proof that he could father a healthy child.

That's when he became an anarchist. A dealer in drugs and flesh. A terrorist. For Nikolai, it was never about the money—although crime was the family trade and he came to enjoy the finer things in life. It was about forcing societal upheaval. Or it had been, until the diagnosis. And now, it was simply about survival.

At the bedside stood a long table filled with illuminated monitors. The property's perimeter was shown from a dozen different angles. At least he'd be warned if someone arrived, although in truth there was no way to stop an assault on the compound.

The phone shivered across the bedside table and trilled. Only one person had this number and he didn't bother to look at the screen for the caller's I D.

"Da," he said. And then in English, for his American contact, *"Yes?"*

"We have a problem," the man began.

"Yes?"

"Two, actually."

"Oh?"

"I just got confirmation, Joe Owens will recover."

Nikolai cursed. It was a problem, just not exactly his problem. "So?"

"So?" the other man barked. "When Joe Owens comes to, he'll have a lot to say. He'll tell them all about the drugs he's been taking and who gave them to him. He'll tell them about the fight and the attack. He'll tell them all about my involvement. If that happens, I won't be able to protect you."

Nikolai grunted a laugh. For decades, he'd been dealing with rough men and lawlessness. This American was nothing. "Don't threaten me, you pissant."

"It's not a threat. But there will be an investigation and it'll be out of my hands."

"What about the woman you were able to frame?" It had been a brilliant stroke of luck that the athlete's agent had shown up when she did. Even more fortuitous that she had seemed sick and the American was wise enough to use her.

"She's another problem altogether."

He waited a beat. "How so?"

"She's working with Ian Wallace. I asked around about him and he's a hotshot private security guy."

Nikolai's breathing echoed in his ears. Ian Wallace. So he was calling himself *private security*. More like a mercenary with a conscience. It explained how he'd been found at his last safe house, and how Yuri Kuzntov and the others had been discovered, as well. How long could he expect to stay safely hidden this time? Days, maybe? Definitely not the weeks or months he needed. They had to tie up all loose ends now.

"Listen carefully," said Nikolai. "Joe Owens can never wake up."

"What are you saying?" the American asked. "You want me to…to kill him? How am I supposed to do that?"

"You're a smart man with connections. You figure something out."

"I'm not a murderer."

"And yet you tried to kill Owens to keep him from going to the media about the experimental drugs you've been providing."

"That was a fight that got out of hand," the American said.

Nikolai laughed. "You stabbed him again and again. If you can do that, you can find a way to kill him that won't leave a trace. No one will suspect if a gravely ill man doesn't recover as hoped."

There was a moment of silence. "Fine, but I won't kill the woman."

"You need to get her away from Ian Wallace. Isolate her for me."

"I can do that," said the American. "Joe Owens's death will give me the perfect excuse to get her by herself. It might take a little while. You need to give me a day or two."

Patience was not a virtue that plagued Nikolai Mateev. He wanted both problems dealt with and now. "You have until morning."

The American didn't thank him for his generosity or understanding. Neither did he end the call.

"Is there more?" Nikolai asked.

"Yeah," said the other man. "I have one question—what do I do with the woman, Petra Sloane, once I have her?"

For Nikolai, the answer to that question was simple. "Bring her to me. I'll make sure she can never go to Ian Wallace for help again."

Chapter 11

Ian's confession about his mentor at MI5 hung in the air, like the last note of a song that was fading away. It was a story he'd never shared with her when they were together. At the same time, Petra knew that he had a past and part of his job was confidential.

Ian slumped in his seat and twirled the empty wineglass.

"You look as exhausted as I feel," she said to Ian.

"Not tired, just thinking."

"About what?"

He shrugged. "Everything."

"Let me help you out a little." She gathered all the dishes from the island and placed them in the sink. "I'll clean up the kitchen and you go and rest."

"Leave it," he said. "The kitchen will keep until the morning."

"With all the surprises today, that might be the most shocking," she said, teasing. "You, ignoring a mess."

Ian stood and stretched. "You think you're funny, don't you?" he teased in return.

"Maybe a little." Petra wiped down the counters and the stove. It was something to keep her hands busy while trying to decide what was right—or wrong.

"I want to look into what your friend Rick said about Arnie Hatch. I'm interested if he invested in big pharmaceuticals—something that might produce performance-enhancing drugs." Ian turned for the door. "Good night, then."

"Wait," she called.

Ian paused and turned to her. "Yes?"

Driven by the need to feel something beyond afraid, she moved to him, felt the heat of his body envelope her. She needed to see that there was still love and joy and beauty in the world, even if it was just for one night. She needed Ian.

And at the same time, she knew that after this, after she was finally safe, it would truly be the end for them. Was there any better way to say goodbye than this?

Reaching for Ian, she splayed her hands across his chest. Through the fine fabric of his shirt, she felt his heartbeat, and hers began to mirror the rhythm.

He gripped both her wrists in one hand and pulled them from his chest. "You don't have to do this."

"I want you. I need you to make love to me. Is there anything wrong with that?"

"It depends on why."

"Stop asking questions and kiss me, before I begin to feel stupid."

"I'm not sure that this is the best idea," said Ian.

She rose to her tiptoes and licked the seam between his lips. "I am."

He cupped her cheek. "I don't want it to complicate things, that's all."

"Tonight's already complicated." She stepped closer, so their bodies were pressed together. He wrapped his arms around her waist, pulling her closer. It had been years since she'd been held, and pleasure rippled across her skin.

Ian cupped her breast and his thumb stroked her nipple into a peak, his fingers branding her flesh. His mouth found hers and he kissed her deeply. "Tell me that you want me," he rasped, his breath stealing her own.

Petra didn't pause to think about what it would mean to surrender to her basest desires. "I want you," she said with a sigh.

With his hands on her waist, Ian turned her around and bent her over the counter. Petra didn't resist. She wanted him to take control, needed to lose herself with him.

"You feel so good," he said, his breath hot on her skin. "I wonder if you taste as good as I remember."

Then, his mouth was on her. She held on to the counter as he suckled her sex, her fingers never gaining purchase on the smooth granite. His tongue explored her most intimate parts. Petra's body slipped away, until all that remained were sensations. Emotions.

Lust and regret. Love and fear.

She cried out with a powerful climax.

"Don't think we're done," he said, his voice thick with lust. "I'm just getting started."

She peered over her shoulder as Ian removed a foil condom packet from his wallet and sheathed himself.

He entered her in one stroke. She gasped as his thrusts deepened. It had always been like this, the need so raw it couldn't wait for the bedroom. Her ecstasy grew, claiming her thoughts, her mind, her soul. Another orgasm shook her body. Ian drove in deep.

As Petra's heart rate returned to normal, she wondered how she was supposed to navigate her feelings for Ian now.

Ian was still inside her—still hard. He pushed his hands through Petra's hair, luxuriating in the feel of the silky strands sliding between his fingers. "Two years is too long."

He thrust once more and spun her around to face him. His lips found hers and he claimed her with his mouth. Her kisses were fiery and began to melt the ice that filled his veins. His shirtfront was open and he stripped down to flesh. Then carefully, he found the hem of her dress and pulled it up slowly, inch by agonizing inch. Exposing her thighs, her hips, her stomach, her breasts. He drank in the sight of her like a man dying of thirst.

He lifted the dress over her head before letting the fabric fall to a heap on the floor. Yet he kept Petra's arms above her head. He intended to hold on to her, to make her his. To love her so well that she'd never leave him, not again.

He pressed his body into her, reaching between her thighs. She was wet and open. He rubbed his thumb over her swollen sex. A moan escaped her throat. "Oh, Ian," she panted, as he increased the pressure.

"You're mine," he said. "And no one else's. Do you hear?"

Her hips were rocking back and forth on his hand. She was close… But he needed to hear the words. "You're mine," he repeated.

She clung to his bare shoulders, her fingernails gouging his skin. "I'm yours, Ian. I love you," she moaned, as he brought her to the pinnacle of ecstasy.

It was enough for him, and the frost that covered his soul began to melt. It was why he loved Petra and needed her in his life. Without her, he felt nothing beyond cold and distant.

He wrapped Petra's legs around his waist. Bracing her against the wall, he entered her. He kept his eyes on her face as he made love to her. The way she parted her lips as she sighed his name. The flush in her cheeks. The way her skin glowed with perspiration. The way her breasts pressed against his chest, and a million other things besides.

The passion between them had always been hot—so hot that they'd gotten burned. But, now that he had her back in his life, Ian wondered if he'd ever be able to let her go a second time.

Chapter 12

The room was awash in rosy light as the sun began to crest the horizon. Petra awoke, naked, in the bed that she and Ian had shared for years. It was almost as if she'd never left, yet to pretend that would be foolish.

She remembered the night it all fell apart. The fight. The hurt. The anger. The tears.

In her memory, she stood next to the kitchen window looking into the backyard. The day had been clear, but cold. Frost turned the dead grass brittle. Inside, the earthy scent of kale sautéed with olive oil and garlic mingled with the spicy aroma of chicken cacciatore. She'd opened a bottle of merlot to accompany their dinner and the decanter sat, untouched, on the island.

But that had been hours ago.

Still staring out the window, Petra scooped another bite from the pan into her mouth. The food had no taste and at the back of her mind was the tingle of fear that came along with the unanswered questions—what if something happened to Ian? What if he was late because he would never make it home again?

She picked up her phone again and sent a new text.

Expected you hours ago. Everything okay?

It was delivered, but not read.

She scrolled through the dozen texts she had sent him since her parents arrived from Cleveland that afternoon.

My parents here. Excited to see you.

Food's getting cold. Almost home?

And the final one: If you aren't coming, lmk.

The front door opened and a blast of frigid air swirled through the kitchen. It was Ian. She waited for him to call to her, to apologize. He did neither. He was on the phone.

"It's solid evidence about Mateev and the DEA. He's in the States…"

Petra quit listening. Using a juice glass, she poured some wine and took a long swallow. Her insides grew artificially warm. Ian came in to the kitchen, wrapped a cold arm around her middle and kissed her cheek.

"Smells good," he said.

She squirmed out of his grasp. "It's cold."

"That's okay," said Ian. "I can heat it up in the microwave."

She finished the wine in one swallow. "Suit yourself."

"You seem upset. Did something happen at work?"

She didn't bother to look in his direction. "No."

"Are you sure? What's the matter, then?"

"I'm fine."

"You don't seem fine."

Petra leaned against the counter and folded her arms over her chest. "You're right. I'm not fine."

Ian stood by the stove and lifted a limp piece of kale from the pan. Oil dripped from the leaf as he stuck it into his mouth and licked his fingers. "So, is it work…"

"It's not work, Ian. It's us. It's you."

"Me? What have I done?" She'd heard him ask the same question dozens—no, hundreds—of times before. It was like a script to a tired drama and they both knew their parts.

"My parents flew in today from Ohio. They came for dinner…" she began. "After waiting around, they gave up and went to the hotel."

She could feel the tears. They were just under the surface—burning her eyes, tightening her chest, leaving her throat raw as they tried to break free.

"Bloody hell, that was today? I forgot. I'm sorry. Why didn't you remind me?"

She clenched her teeth. "I did. This morning. Yesterday. The day before that."

He opened his mouth, to apologize—explain that he didn't have regular hours, or a regular job. Petra held up her hand. "I don't want your excuses, Ian. I've heard them all before and that's the entire problem. You've done nothing. You haven't called me to say you're late. You haven't answered any one of my dozen texts. You haven't even apologized for standing up my parents."

His jaw was slack. "You know this happens."

Petra hurled the glass in her hand. It hit the wall behind Ian's head, shattering and staining the wall red.

"What the hell? I'm late, I'm sorry, but I thought you knew what I did. I thought you understood."

And suddenly she did understand. "This isn't what I want, Ian. I want to matter enough that my boyfriend will text me back. Or here's a crazy idea—maybe he'll even show up on time."

"My job is important. What I do matters and I'm closer to getting Mateev than ever."

"Mateev. It's always Mateev. What is this guy to you?" The tears had come and she had no way to stop them now. "I know your job matters. But I want to matter, too. This isn't working."

"What's not working?"

"Us. I think I need to leave."

"Do not threaten me."

But Petra was beyond making threats. In fact, she no longer cared. "I just can't, Ian. I can't do this anymore."

Without a reply, he turned and left her alone in the

kitchen. She remained by the counter, a dirty fork cradled to her chest. How different would things have been if she'd gone after him?

And then she was back in the bedroom with Ian beside her, just like it had been before. In fact, it was exactly as it had been before. They still shared passion. Yet Ian still served a higher purpose: justice.

His dedication to that end had grown and now he was willing to kill.

She was a fool to think that life would be different if she came back—if she had the choice and wasn't convicted of attempted murder and sent to jail.

Petra rolled to face Ian. The blankets were draped low across his torso. His pecs were well-defined and covered in a sprinkling of blond hair. His abs were tight, muscles clearly outlined beneath his tanned skin.

She drank in the sight of him, memorized every inch of his body.

His eyes opened, and a slow smile spread across his face. "Morning," he said.

Petra reached up and stroked his face. His skin was warm and stubble covered his cheeks and chin. "Morning."

"I do miss you, Petra," he said.

She'd wanted to hear those words from him since the day their relationship ended. Yet she was no longer content to live her life waiting for Ian to come home from who knew where or close his latest assignment. She needed more. She had changed. The question was, had he?

"Ian," she said, pulling the sheet over her, "we need to talk."

"That doesn't sound good."

Petra paused, not sure what she wanted to say, much less how to say it. Before she could voice her thoughts, there was a loud knock on the front door. She glanced at the bedside clock. It was six thirty. "Someone stopping by this early isn't good, either," she said.

"Wait here," Ian said.

He slipped from the bed and the muscles in his back flexed as he pulled on a pair of jeans. "I'll be right back." Shirtless and barefoot, he padded across the floor.

Petra stayed where she lay, her breath trapped in her chest. Did this have anything to do with her? Or maybe it was Joe? Had he regained consciousness— and if so, what did he remember?

Petra heard another knock coming from below and then the soft clicking as the door was unlocked and the tumblers fell into place. Ian's voice carried clearly up the stairs.

"Kind of early to stop by," he said. "I take it that you have news."

The question was answered by a man; that much was obvious by the deep rumbling voice. But he spoke softly and she couldn't make out his words.

Ian cursed.

Petra's chest contracted as if squeezed by a vise. She exhaled. Her eyes burned. She slipped from the bed and rummaged through Ian's drawers, selecting a pair of flannel lounge pants and a baggy T-shirt. After pulling them on, she crept to the door and peered over the banister. Ian stood in the entry, holding the door open. On the threshold was Luis Martinez.

"I'm sorry to be the bearer of bad news, Ian," Martinez was saying. "Joe passed away last night. Petra's been charged with murder. I have to take her in, and she won't get bail."

Her. She. Martinez meant Petra. Arrested? It was too much to think about. Her head swam and she gripped the hallway railing to keep upright. The side of her head began to pound. Her stomach roiled and cold sweat covered her skin. The voices rang out, booming yet indistinct.

She couldn't deal with being taken to jail and experiencing a migraine at the same time. She staggered back to the bedroom and dumped the contents of her handbag onto the bedspread. Mascara. Keys. Lipstick. Wallet. Her prescription bottle.

With trembling fingers, she pried the lid open and took out a pill. She stuck it on the back of her tongue and swallowed. The pill burned as it scraped down her dry throat. She stood, sweeping her belongings into a pile at the center of the bed.

Ian appeared at the door. He held the frame, his muscular arms stretched over his head. His bare chest was so broad, those abs above his low-hanging jeans so toned… As she studied his body and all the places she had kissed and touched, she knew that she was avoiding his face and the look of pity she'd certainly see there.

"Petra," he said. His voice was soft and quiet, not a whisper, but holding the hint of a secret ready to be told.

"It's Martinez," she said. "I heard."

"What did you hear?" he asked.

"Enough. I guess I have to go." Her gaze lifted to his face. His eyes were moist. Her throat burned. Maybe it was the pill. She looked away.

"I'm sorry," he said.

"About Joe? He was a good guy. It's a shame that he died, especially when we thought he was improving."

"No, I'm sorry that I haven't haven't found the real attacker. That I haven't been able to clear your name."

"Ian, I told you," said Petra, her voice cracking. "What if it's me?"

Ian shook his head. "No. I'm not going to lose you as soon as you came back into my life. And I'm not letting that cop take you into custody. Get dressed. I'm taking you to an RMJ safe house and then we can plan our next move."

"Are you crazy? How will becoming a fugitive from justice solve anything?"

Ian exhaled. "Do you trust your lawyer?"

"He's expensive. Does that count?"

"Give him a call and get him over here now. I'll keep Martinez busy."

"What if my lawyer tells me to surrender to the police?"

"Then I'll knock Martinez out and lock him in a closet," said Ian.

Petra folded her arms across her chest. "That's not very funny."

"Don't make me beg," said Ian.

"It wouldn't do any good anyhow."

Ian cursed. "Get dressed and call your lawyer. And don't come down until your counsel shows up."

For a moment, her mind was thrust back to Joe's house, as she had stood by his pool. She felt the heat of the day warm her skin and the sun blind her. There were two drinks on the table, the glasses sweaty and ice floating on the surface.

She reached up and touched her head. The bruise at the back of her scalp was still there. She had been hit from behind, because there was one other person at Joe's house when she arrived.

Petra dressed in a pair of jeans and a rust colored T-shirt, before sitting on the bed to slip into her shoes. The phone lay atop the pile from her purse, the screen glowing with an incoming text. It was from Rick Albright: We need to talk. New info. Super important.

Petra glanced at the door and then back at the phone. She sent a quick message.

Can't talk now. Joe died last night and cops are here. I think my memories are coming back. Need to call my lawyer. Will text later.

Rick texted back immediately: Cops? Martinez?

Petra: Yes.

Rick: Be careful

There had been two people at Joe's house. Martinez had been the first to arrive. Yet he had an alibi, or so he said. And wasn't it odd that Martinez had found her here, instead of waiting at her condo?

There was obviously more to Martinez's story.

Petra: Why?

Rick: Did he bring backup or is he alone?

Petra began to tremble again. She sent another message. Tell me what you know.

Rick: Do not go anywhere with that man. He's the one who tried to kill Joe.

Petra: Hold on. I'm going to grab Ian.

Rick: NO!!!! You just have to leave. Martinez is a dangerous man. He's dirty.

Petra: I'm calling the other cops. They need to take care of this.

Rick: NO!!!

Petra: Ian, then. I'll call you in a minute.

Rick: Don't. You'll put everyone's life in danger.

Petra: ???

Rick: Martinez is dangerous. He works for a Russian named Nikolai Mateev.

Nikolai Mateev. It was a name she knew, but only because of Ian. And Martinez was working with the king of Russian organized crime? Her stomach churned, boiling with acid.

Petra recalled the crime scene at Joe's house and froze. There'd been dozens of cops and crime scene technicians. It was more than a little odd that Martinez hadn't brought other police officers—or maybe witnesses?—with him. She'd been mistaken about Martinez. He hadn't come to arrest her for a crime he'd committed. He intended to kill her, thus silencing her forever.

Another text came in and Petra read: You have to get out of the house without causing a scene. Just sneak away.

Petra: I can't. My car's in the driveway. There's no way I can leave without Martinez knowing.

Rick: You have to get out. You aren't safe. I'll come and get you. Meet me in five minutes.

He texted a street address that was two blocks away. Petra's heart raced, thumping in her chest, making her T-shirt flutter. She took in a deep breath. One. Two. Three. Exhale.

In a quiet corner of her mind, Petra knew there were two questions to be answered. First, how could she get out of the house unnoticed? And second, what should she do about Ian?

If Martinez really was working for Nikolai Mateev, then he was far more dangerous than either of them had suspected and that meant they needed backup. The police. The FBI. Or better yet, the old crew from RMJ. All it would take was a phone call once she got out of the house…

She shut and locked the door and then leaned on the wall. Now she needed a way to escape.

Her eyes were drawn to the window. She opened the shades and bright Colorado sunshine flooded the room. She pressed her face to the glass and looked down. It was two stories to the ground, maybe fifteen feet, by her estimation. Farther than she'd dropped at Nikolai Mateev's apartment building, but not by much.

She tucked the phone into her back pocket. She opened the window and removed the four metal brackets that held the screen in place. With it set aside, Petra sat on the windowsill with her legs dangling. From here it looked a lot farther to the ground than her original guess had been.

Yet she had no choice.

Maybe this wasn't the best idea. Certainly, if she went downstairs, she could find a way to quietly warn Ian and then, together, they could get away from Martinez.

Backing out of the window, Petra hung by her

fingers. Finally, stretched out long, she let go. The weightless feeling nauseated her and then her feet hit the grass.

Petra sprinted down the street, all the while fighting the urge to look over her shoulder. What would Martinez do if he saw her running away? She imagined a set of crosshairs tattooed onto her flesh. She pushed her legs harder.

From half a block away she saw a red sedan idling at a stop sign, and she pulled up short. Who else was watching her? Who else was waiting? Then she remembered Rick had been in an accident and now drove a rental car.

Petra dashed the last hundred yards, her side cramping with the exertion. Breathing hard, she came up to the car. Rick leaned across the console to open the passenger door.

At least she was away from Martinez and with someone she could trust. Now to call in the professionals. "Thanks for coming to get me, Rick," she said, by way of greeting. "I remember something from Joe's. There were two glasses on his patio. They both had ice cubes in them, so they hadn't been there long. Which means that whoever was there with him, whoever attacked him, was still at the house."

"Get in," Rick said. "We can talk about it further once we get you away from Martinez."

Petra felt a flush creep up her face. She should've known better than to stand outside gabbing. She slipped into the car and shut the door. Using the automatic lock, Rick secured the door. He stepped on the accelerator and the sedan shot forward.

Rick slammed the heel of his hand into the steering wheel twice. "I can't believe this is happening, Petra. It's all so messed up."

His reaction surprised her and she watched him as he drove. His complexion was dull and the bruises on his face had turned from purples and blues to yellows and greens. The cut to his lip was scabbed over, but his mouth was still swollen. Even though she'd seen him the day before, he looked worse.

But it wasn't just his injuries.

There was something wrong. Though she could feel cold air blasting out of the vents, a sheen of sweat covered Rick's forehead. Beyond the new-car smell and the sweat, there was something else. It was sour and dank, like vinegar or curdled milk.

Was it sickness? No, she decided, it was fear.

What was Rick afraid of?

He rounded a corner and pulled in to an undeveloped cul-de-sac, where there was nothing beyond the curb but open fields of scrub.

"I should call Ian right now," said Petra, as she pulled up his contact information. "Just to let him know where I've gone." Her finger hovered over the call icon. A thought came to her, and it was like finding a puzzle piece that she didn't even know was missing. "How do you know about Nikolai Mateev?"

"What do you mean?"

"You said that Martinez was working for Nikolai Mateev, a Russian gangster."

"He is," said Rick, "which is why you had to get out of there."

The sour and spoiled scent came again, and she knew where she'd smelled it before. "It was you," she said. "You were at Joe's, and then at my apartment last night."

"I don't know what you're talking about," Rick said.

"You were there, Rick. Admit it."

Rick opened his mouth, then clamped it shut. "It didn't have to be this way, Petra."

"You're too good of a guy to be tangled up in whatever you're doing…" She sprang for the door, her only means of escape. She pulled up on the handle with her free hand.

It wouldn't budge.

Rick grabbed her other wrist, his fingers biting into her flesh. Her hand went numb and the phone fell from her grasp. It landed on her lap, before tumbling to the floorboard—taking away her link to the outside world.

She dived for Rick, remembering the wound she'd given him last night. Her fist connected with his middle. He doubled over with a curse. She reached for the lock and pulled it up. Grabbing the handle, she pushed the door open. He yanked her arm and a burning pain shot through her shoulder as he nearly tore it from the socket. She twisted and kicked as best she could, but Rick pulled her straight back.

Rick held a cloth in his hand. He pressed down, covering her nose and mouth. Fumes surrounded her, making her eyes water and her throat constrict. She pushed Rick's hand away. The cloth came down harder on her face.

Petra's thoughts became a jumble—nothing more than leaves in a windstorm. She pushed at the hand that held her one more time, and then Petra forgot why she had even bothered to fight in the first place.

Chapter 13

Ian lifted the cup to his lips and paused. A film floated on the top of the tepid tea and clung to the sides of the cup. He set it on the counter without taking a sip.

Martinez leaned against the wall and consulted a fitness tracker at his wrist. "Any idea when Petra will come down? I don't want this to get ugly, but I will forcibly remove her from the house, if necessary."

It had been nearly thirty minutes since Martinez had arrived and Ian didn't know how much longer they'd need to wait for the attorney.

"I'll be right back," said Ian, as he left the kitchen.

He needed to speak to Petra. If her expensive attorney wasn't going to do his job, then they needed another plan. He loved her too much to let her go.

His steps faltered. He loved Petra, and no matter what, she was what mattered—not Nikolai Mateev, not the Russian mob, not promises he'd made fifteen years ago, not even his career or RMJ.

Ian took the stairs two at a time. He strode up the final steps and stopped at the bedroom door. He gave a sharp knock. "Petra? It's me. Can I come in?"

She didn't answer. He knocked again, louder this time. "Petra?"

Still there was no reply.

He reached for the handle and jerked it up and down. It held fast. Ian slapped the flat of his hand on the door. "Petra. Open up."

"Everything okay?" Martinez stood in the foyer, looking up.

A million different catastrophes came to Ian at once. Petra, in the midst of a migraine, incapacitated and sprawled on the floor. A fall in the bathroom and a subsequent head injury. The metallic taste of panic coated Ian's tongue. "Petra?"

Martinez was at his side—Ian had been so focused that he hadn't even noticed the large cop coming up the stairs. "Ms. Sloane? It's Detective Sergeant Martinez. I need you to open the door."

Nothing.

Leg cocked, Ian kicked the lock. There was a crack as wood splintered and metal bent and twisted. The door tilted and swung inward. Ian pushed his way into the room, Martinez right behind him. The window was open and the screen leaned against the wall. Ian's gut dropped to his shoes. Petra was gone.

A pair of his sleep pants and a T-shirt lay in a heap on the bedroom floor. A dresser drawer hung open, the few clothes inside askew, instead of folded neatly. Petra's handbag lay on the bed, the contents scattered about.

"She got dressed," Ian said, aloud. "Then dumped her purse out and left through the window. But why?"

"Easy," said Martinez. "She didn't want to go to jail."

Ian lifted the purse and looked at what Petra had left behind. Wallet. Sunglasses. Car keys. Lipstick. No phone. Who had she called to ask for help? Who had she trusted more than him? Ian carefully set the purse down, his hand lingering on the soft leather.

With the force of a sledgehammer, the betrayal hit him in the chest. The pain was excruciating and quick, gone as soon as it came. Yet Ian could feel it—a piece of his heart had broken off and he would never be whole again. If Martinez hadn't been standing next to him, he would have laughed at himself for playing the fool.

How could he have cared for Petra again? Damn it, he'd fallen in love with her a second time.

For a moment, he considered simply letting Petra go and make her own way. That was obviously what she wanted, and he shouldn't have expected any less. Wasn't that what she did best when things became difficult—run?

Certainly, Martinez was a resourceful cop and would eventually track her down. He didn't need Ian's help, didn't need to know that Petra's phone was missing, or that Ian had the ability to track the number.

Yet maybe Ian needed to face her duplicity head-on, needed to see Petra one last time, and then properly say goodbye.

"If you know where she is," said Martinez, "you're bound to tell me, unless you want to face charges for aiding and abetting."

Ian grunted. After all the laws he'd broken recently, a few more didn't matter.

Martinez must've decided to try again, use a different tactic. "I can tell you care for Petra. And if you do, you need to help her. The longer she's on the run the worse it will be once she's caught. You know that."

Ian nodded slowly. He knew what Martinez said was true, and still he felt like a heel. "I can find her," he said. "Come with me."

In his office, Ian used his desktop to open the Rocky Mountain Justice site. From there, he found the second number listed under his name. He highlighted it and opened the phone's app. A list of texts recently sent and received appeared. They were all to and from Rick Albright, the team physician.

Did Ian even know Petra anymore? He glanced at the first text and his insides turned icy.

"What the hell?" Martinez muttered, while reading over Ian's shoulder. "That's not right. I'm not working with Nikolai Mateev."

Where Ian's gut had been frozen before, it now filled with molten fury. Nikolai Mateev was not a name most people—even police officers—should recognize. How was Martinez involved? Had Ian been duped? Was he now helping the enemy?

"But you do know Nikolai Mateev."

"I wouldn't say that I know him."

"What would you say, then?"

"I've heard the name, that's all. The FBI gave the Detectives' Bureau a briefing about him and the possibility that he's in the state. Something went down in Boulder, but the details were sketchy. We were ordered to turn all our information over to the Feds."

"Who briefed you?"

"I don't know," said Martinez. He held his hands up in surrender. "It was months ago."

"Try to remember," Ian urged. He wasn't entirely sure if Martinez was to be trusted.

"Well…" The detective paused and scratched the back of his head. "He was a bigwig out of the Denver field office. A bald guy. Jones, or maybe Johnson."

The answer made sense, as did Martinez's reaction of disbelief and nervousness. "Jones," said Ian. "Special Agent Marcus Jones. He hired my firm, Rocky Mountain Justice, to find Mateev."

"Then you know more about this than I do."

Ian decided to trust Martinez, if for no other reason than he had no choice. "If you aren't working with Nikolai Mateev, it brings up an interesting question. How does Rick Albright know his name?"

Ian's question was followed by silence. The answer was simple and obvious. Rick Albright had been the key all along. He was the one who had attacked Joe Owens, and then Petra in her own home. Rick

Albright was in league with Nikolai Mateev, one of the most dangerous men in the world. And now he had Petra.

Nikolai Mateev lay on the bed with an IV attached to his arm. A bag of fluid was held up by a pole and clear medication dripped through the tube. His veins filled with warmth. It flooded his body, returning his strength and vitality and washing away his exhaustion.

Rick Albright, the doctor Mateev had bought and paid for, stood next to the IV and checked the tubing. "How are you feeling?" he asked.

"Better than I have in years," said Nikolai. "Although that's not saying much."

The doctor, clad in a golf shirt and jeans, removed the needle from his arm and taped a gauze pad over the open puncture mark. He stripped off a pair of latex gloves and threw them into a nearby wastebasket. "Just remember that the energy you're feeling from the treatment will last for seven to eight days. It will slowly begin to fade, and you'll grow weaker as that happens. Then in a month, you can have another session."

Nikolai nodded. He knew that this treatment was experimental, temporary and illegal. Yet none of that mattered. He'd heard that some of his heroin was being used as a performance-enhancing drug in Colorado. Desperate for relief, Mateev wondered what the performance enhancer might do to someone who was ill.

He had traveled to the US to find out.

In order to avoid the authorities, Nikolai had changed everything about his life. He lived in modest homes and was driven in cheap cars. It was far from the palace he owned outside of Saint Petersburg or the high-rise penthouse in Moscow. He missed his old life of wealth and power.

Then again, what was luxury to a corpse?

For the most part, Mateev had been able to move about the state without raising any suspicion. And all the hardships had been worth it. The medication, developed by Dr. Albright to make athletes stronger, faster and more agile, was truly magical. These past eight weeks, Nikolai had more energy than he'd had five years prior—even before his diagnosis.

Like Lazarus, he had risen from the grave.

"What do you plan to do with her?" the doctor asked. He flipped a hand to the motionless woman on the floor.

Nikolai's hospital bed had been placed in the middle of a warehouse. High windows were covered with years of grime and let in scant sun. A single lightbulb hung from the ceiling. The artificial light was insufficient for such a large space, and the woman, who was less than twenty feet from the bed, was all but lost in the gloom.

Ilya and Anatoly sat on folding chairs at a plastic table. Each held a hand of cards, and the rest of the deck was between them.

Mateev looked at the woman. Her long hair fanned out on the floor. Even with her head turned to the side, he knew she was the person who had found his last apartment. "Wake her," Mateev said to the doctor. "I need to find out what she knows about Ian Wallace and what he knows about me."

Albright looked away. "I don't think it's much. Petra only hired him to help her find out what happened at Joe Owens's house."

Nikolai read the doctor's hesitancy as an emotional attachment to the woman. He sniffed. An ache shot through his abdomen. He gritted his teeth and ignored the pain, ignored the tumor that grew inside his body, ignored the burning in his veins.

"The woman was staying at Ian's house. She is hardly a *sluchaynyy kliyent*." He translated for the American. "*Random client. Besides, what happens when her memories return? She'll know that she didn't attack Joe Owens, and could very well remember your presence." Nikolai continued, "Now that I've gotten my treatment, we can leave Denver and return to Moscow."

"Suit yourself," said Albright. "I need to get back to the stadium. There's a staff meeting."

"You misunderstand, my doctor friend. You'll be coming to Russia with me. Now, in fact."

Albright blanched. "This wasn't part of our agreement."

"It wasn't," agreed Mateev. He didn't know how long he could stay hidden from Ian Wallace in America, which meant he had to return to Russia. "But the situation has changed and our agreement must change, as well."

"No way, no how," said Albright.

"You don't want to disappoint me, Doctor. I don't take well to being turned down."

"You can threaten me all you want. I'm not giving up my life in Colorado to go to Russia with you."

"You understand that your other option is to lose your life altogether," said Mateev.

Ilya looked up from his game of cards and placed a gun on the table—the threat made clear.

"You think you scare me?" Albright's voice rose two octaves, becoming a schoolgirl shrill.

"I terrify you," said Mateev. "Or at least I should. Nobody gets a chance to say no to me twice."

The doctor separated the IV pole into four sections and tucked them into an open medical kit at his feet. He wrapped the tubing around one hand and slipped it into the brown leather case, as well. The silence was bravado, Albright's way of retaining some control of the situation. It mattered only a little to Mateev. In the end, the doctor would agree.

"My services won't be cheap," he finally said. "Giving up a home, a job, a life, in order to help you will cost a pretty penny."

"I have several pennies," said Mateev, "pretty and otherwise. Name your price."

"Seven million in US dollars per year," said Albright. "I also want a nice apartment in Moscow."

Mateev would have paid ten times that amount without hesitation. He was amazed at the naïveté of the doctor—and was happy to take advantage of him. "Done," he said. "We leave after I speak to the woman. Wake her up."

Albright crouched before his medical bag and snapped the closure shut. "I can't do that. I used chloroform. It needs time to wear off."

"How long?"

Albright shrugged. "Every patient is different. Another hour. Maybe two."

"We could bring her with us," Anatoly suggested. "She can be questioned on a plane as easily as she can be questioned in this warehouse."

"There are too many things that can go wrong with transporting a hostage. I want to know everything that she knows and then I want her dead before we leave," Mateev stated coldly.

Albright gave a strangled, gurgling sound. "Dead? Why kill her? If we're gone, then she's no longer a threat."

"Now you care for her well-being? Where was your concern when you framed her for a crime that you committed?"

"I took an oath to heal. I just don't like the idea of having more blood on my hands, that's all."

"You also took a good amount of my money. I fear that you have mistaken my generosity for kindness," said Mateev. "Let us make something plain. I own you."

The doctor crouched in front of his bag and rewrapped the tubing before tucking it in tight.

"Nothing to say?" Mateev asked. "No clever retort?"

Albright had the sense to silently tend to his medical kit.

Nikolai mumbled, *"Chto za pridurok." What a jerk.*

With his question of how he would continue to receive his medical treatments answered, he was ready to leave. Not just the warehouse or the state, but the entire country. America was no friend of his.

It had taken the life of his only son, kept him from his grandson and much of his business was left in tatters. Once he was back in Russia, Nikolai could begin rebuilding his empire.

Still, he felt like a wounded animal and wanted to return to his den and lick his wounds. Remaining in America for even another hour stretched out like a year.

"Get a jet here," he said.

"Sure thing," said Ilya. "When do you want to leave?"

"Now," said Nikolai.

"What about the woman?"

Back to that tiresome question. Maybe it was best to kill her before she even woke. Even on a private jet, Nikolai didn't want to deal with transporting a prisoner or disposing of a corpse while traveling. At the same time, he refused to sit and wait for her to come to. Then again, would Ian Wallace follow him to Russia?

"We have no choice," he said. "Bring her with us."

He sat up and dropped his feet to the floor. He stood. A coating of cold sweat covered his skin. The floor underfoot seemed to tilt. Pinpricks of light danced in his vision. He gripped the side of the bed, waiting for his eyesight to return. When it did, he wiped a shaking hand across his damp brow.

Dr. Albright was on his feet and at Nikolai's side. He placed his hand on Nikolai's elbow. "Maybe you should sit back down and let the medication take effect. This is a new dosage and we don't know how you'll react."

Nikolai brushed him away. "Don't presume to touch me," he said. "Do what you need to do so we can leave." He looked at his bodyguard and driver, both still at the table with the card game between them. "All of you," he snarled, "now."

A map of Denver filled the computer screen. Ian placed his finger over a pulsating green dot. A spark warmed his skin, as if he was really touching Petra. "That's where she is."

He sat back and changed the aspect, compressing the picture until the street names came into view.

Martinez gave a low whistle. "Hell, that's out of the city and halfway to Greeley. Nothing's there but an abandoned industrial park. No one around to get suspicious. Sounds like the perfect place to take a kidnapping victim."

Bile rose in the back of Ian's throat. He'd been on the job too long to hope that things were going well for Petra. In fact, he might even be too late to save her. That thought landed in his brain like an exploding bomb. The pain stole his breath. Ian pressed the heels of his hands into his eye sockets, until there was nothing for him to see other than darkness and circulating blood.

He stood. His chair rolled back, hitting the wall. "I'm going after her," he said to himself.

Still, Martinez answered, "We should get in touch with your contact from the Feds."

Ian tried to image that phone call to Special Agent Jones. It would take hours to convince Jones to act—that was, if Ian wasn't arrested first. "You call your people and see what you can make happen. Someone will need to clean up afterward."

"You can't be saying that you're going after Nikolai Mateev alone?"

Ian shook his head. "I don't care about Mateev anymore. I'm going to rescue Petra."

"It might be a recovery," said Martinez.

Ian had thought the same thing, yet to hear someone confirm his worst fears made his stomach churn. His mouth filled with acid. He clenched his teeth. "She's not dead."

"Either way, you can't go after her alone."

Ian opened his mouth, ready to argue. But just then the computer screen went black and a two-word command appeared: Program Complete. The contents he'd copied from the laptop recovered from the Comrades' safe house had finally been opened.

Dropping into the chair, Ian unlocked the program. A list of files appeared on the screen. Dozens of them. Hundreds. Dare he guess a thousand? Bank accounts. Routes for the drug trade. The home addresses of other gangsters. All of it was here, and now Ian knew everything there was to know about Mateev.

But he couldn't just leave it sitting on his computer,

doing nothing. And if he took his time to analyze the data, he'd never find Petra. He'd been a fool to fire everyone at RMJ. Now more than ever he needed his team. His family.

And yet he did have Martinez.

"This—" Ian pointed to the screen "—is all the information you'll ever need to bring down the entire Russian mob, and the American mob, and who knows what else. Copy it to a flash drive. Say it came to you from an anonymous source and then give it to Special Agent Jones. You'll be the most famous cop in the country."

"No way," said Martinez. "If this Rick Albright guy killed Joe Owens, then I'm going after him. Joe was my friend and I owe him whatever justice I can deliver."

Ian didn't have time to argue. At least there was one person left in the RMJ offices. He placed a call. "Katarina," he said as soon as the ringing stopped. His fingers danced along the keys as he sent all the documents to Katarina. "I'm emailing you something now. Copy it to a flash drive and get it to Jones."

He hit Send.

"I'm on the computer now." Her words were drawn out, hesitant. "I got it. Anything else?"

"Sure," said Ian. "Wish me luck. I'm going to need it."

"Good luck," she said, without asking anything more.

Ian ended the call and strode to the hallway, Martinez at his side. "If you come with me," said Ian, "we're going in alone. I don't have time for police procedures or intel gathering or any of that."

"I get it," said the detective.

Growing up in England was vastly different than growing up in America for many reasons—and one of them was guns. In England, your fists and your wits got you both into and out of trouble. And using a gun during a crime got you sent to jail for the better part of your life. In fact, MI5 didn't even give agents guns and Ian had never learned to rely on them.

But today was different. Today, he would use any weapon he had.

Ian had his personal Walther, which he slid into a shoulder holster and covered as he donned a leather jacket. He wished like hell that he had more firepower. But going to another RMJ safehouse to raid the arsenal would take more time than he was willing to expend.

He could call Roman and Cody and Julia, ask them to collect some guns and then meet him at the warehouse. And yet he had treated them all poorly. Would they be willing to help after he had lied to them?

Chapter 14

Petra's head throbbed. It was a more intense pain than she'd ever experienced. Her lips were dry, her tongue felt like cotton in her mouth. She tried to open her eyes and look around, but her lids felt as if they'd been glued shut. She could tell that it was dark. Was it night? Or was she simply in a room with no lights? She lay without moving and reached for any memories. They floated in a mist, just out of her grasp.

She took inventory of her body. She hurt everywhere, and yet nothing was unbearable. Petra took that as a good sign. The stench of gasoline and motor oil and rot hung about her like a fog. She lay on something hard and cold. A cement floor.

Had she had another migraine and passed out? She inhaled. One. Two. Three.

As she exhaled, Petra remembered everything. Joe mysteriously dying overnight in the hospital. Martinez showing up at Ian's with an arrest warrant in hand. Rick's texts, luring her to apparent safety—and his attack.

It was all Rick Albright. He'd done this to her. But why?

Petra's ears began buzzing. Then the noise morphed into words. She heard two distinct male voices. Yet for some reason—one she couldn't explain—Petra felt that there were more than two men nearby.

"Sure thing," said one man. He had an Eastern European accent. Russian? "When do you want to leave?"

"Now," said the other man. He had a similar accent, yet it wasn't as heavy as the first. His voice was deeper. Slower. From his intonation, she guessed that he was the older of the two.

"What about the woman?"

The woman? Did he mean her? Petra gasped and the men fell silent. She didn't want them to know she was awake, not until she had time to assess the situation. Had they heard her? Panic gripped her chest, forcing the breath from her lungs.

The older man spoke again. "We have no choice. Bring her with us."

She began to breathe again as a thousand questions flooded her thoughts. Take her with them where? And what did they plan to do with her?

She had to get out of here. But where was she? And how could she get help?

She opened her eyes a fraction. A single bulb hung from the ceiling above her, illuminating a hospital bed and a table with folding chairs. Four men stood about fifteen feet away. Too far for her to see them clearly, and hopefully, vice versa.

Both Petra's arms were splayed out at her sides. She moved one slowly, inch by inch, to her back pocket, where she'd put her phone, but found nothing there. Then she recalled it slipping from her grasp as she fought Rick in his sedan. That meant she was on her own, and if she wanted to escape, she had to do it herself.

She opened her eyes further. The men—two younger, one older, and Rick—stood around the bed. One of the younger men had a phone to his ear. "We can get a plane into the private terminal at Denver International Airport by seven o'clock."

"Too long," said the older man. He stood with his back to Petra, yet something about him looked familiar.

"We need the right people on staff to avoid customs…" the first man said.

"Find the right people."

The man returned to his call, speaking in a language Petra didn't understand but was almost certain was Russian. "If we can get to Colorado Springs in ninety minutes, there's a supervisor that won't look too closely at passports."

"How much?" asked the older man.

"He wants twenty thousand US dollars, Nikolai."

Nikolai? As in Nikolai Mateev? Petra's stomach

bucked and threatened to empty. If Nikolai Mateev had arranged her kidnapping, Petra was as good as dead. Unless she could get away.

"I almost hate it when they come so cheap," Nikolai said. "It's like they're too stupid to know what to ask for, which means I'm working with an idiot." He paused. "Done."

The younger man spoke into the phone, and the older one turned his head to the side and she saw him in profile. Petra went cold. The same man who had thrown her over the railing. The one from Ian's photo. Nikolai Mateev.

The men talked more about the logistics of their trip, not paying any attention to Petra. It suited her just fine. Every minute counted. Using the heels of her hands and her knees, she scooted backward. Once. Twice.

She dared to lift her head and look over her shoulder, though not for long. Yet she'd seen enough to know that the room was endless, almost the size of a football field, with high windows and no sign of a door. Twenty feet behind her were metal drums meant to hold sixty gallons of liquid, lined up in rows or stacked one atop the next. The towers reached thirty feet into the air and left Petra with the impression of being lost in an industrial forest.

Lifting herself in a crouch, she half scooted, half crawled to the nearest drum and dropped out of sight. Her heart pounded and her breath came short and ragged. She sat still and silent until her pulse slowed. Then she inhaled and listened to the men talking, their voices now nothing more than rumbles of distant thunder.

Petra surveyed her surroundings. The next drum was more than ten feet to her left. In front of her was a wall of metal containers that almost reached the ceiling, blocking her view of anything else—namely a way out. She looked at the windows. Sunshine struggled in through grime-coated glass, allowing diffused light to linger at the top of the room. If she could find the windows, she could find the walls. It also meant that Petra could eventually find the door—and freedom.

She peered around the drum, scanning the room quickly for an illuminated exit sign. There was none, not that she thought it would be that easy. All the same, she had hoped. Her plan, such that it was, was simple. Get as far away from Nikolai and Rick as possible. Find a door. Escape.

She looked at the next drum over. She inhaled. One. Two. Exhale. Go.

Keeping low, she ran.

"Hey!" one of the men shouted.

Petra instinctively dropped down, lying flat on the floor. Her heart ceased to beat. She dared not move, look toward the man who had called out or even breathe.

"Where'd she go?" he asked. It was one of the younger Russians; she could tell by his accent. "The woman's gone."

"Gone?" asked Nikolai Mateev. "Well, go and find her. And then bring her to me."

* * *

Ian Wallace pulled his SUV to the shoulder of the frontage road. The car idled as waves of heat shimmered off the hood. A haze of smog and dust hung in the air, turning the world to faded sepia. He was northeast of Denver, the Rocky Mountains at his back. The Great Plains stretched out before him.

He looked through a pair of binoculars at a complex of abandoned warehouses. It was the size of a small town. Set up in rows, the metal buildings were coated with khaki-colored dust. The road through the center of the complex, long neglected, bucked and bowed with broken asphalt. A few scraggly trees grew near a sagging chain-link fence and a tumbleweed bounced along in the breeze. Already, nature was reclaiming this desolate stretch of land.

He handed the binocs to Martinez, who peered through them and spoke as he surveyed the property. "It doesn't look like anyone's been here in years."

Yet they both knew that wasn't true. The GPS in Petra's phone had led them right here.

"Will you look at that," said Martinez. He handed the binoculars back to Ian. "Just beside the gate. See the yellow sign, right below the No Trespassing one?"

Ian scanned the fencing. He found what Martinez wanted him to see—and he immediately knew why. "Property of Hatch Enterprises. I assume that's Arnie Hatch, owner of the Colorado Mustangs."

"You'd assume right," Martinez said.

Ian didn't care about corrupt businessmen—not when Petra's life was on the line. Obviously, Arnie

Hatch was a problem to be dealt with, but later and by other people. He returned his thoughts to Petra, and how best to rescue her.

"What bothers me most is the approach," Ian said. "The whole complex is open. If there are guards, they'll see us the minute we turn off the road. If they have a sharpshooter, we'll be dead before getting to the gate."

"So where does that leave us, General?"

Ian chuckled. "I'm English, you know. It should be Field Marshal."

It was Martinez's turn to chuckle. "You're in America now, my friend. That makes you a general."

General. Field marshal. They were both supreme commanders, which meant it was their job to lead the troops and decide on battle plans. And there was no question in Ian's mind that he was at war. "There are two strategies that will work here. First is stealth and the second is overwhelming power. We have neither."

Ian's phone sat on the console between the seats. He picked it up and flipped it over and over in his hands. He should have made the call before now. But he hadn't… "It leaves us with a single option," he continued. "A frontal assault. It could be suicide, so you don't have to come."

"I'm going to be there when Joe's murderer is arrested. In fact, I'm going to slap on the cuffs and read that piece of garbage his rights."

"This is serious," Ian said. "We don't know who is in that warehouse or what kind of weapons they have. You and I have a couple of handguns, and I can't ask you to risk your life. You stay here and call in backup."

"And miss all the fun?" Martinez pulled his sidearm from a holster at his hip. He retracted the slide and chambered a round. "Besides, who wants to live forever?"

Ian nodded and opened his contact list. He selected a name and made a call. It automatically went through the in-car phone system. A single ring came through the SUV's speakers before being answered.

"I didn't think I'd hear from you," Roman said, not bothering with any pleasantries.

Ian ignored the hostile tone and the brusque words. "You're on speaker and I have Detective Sergeant Luis Martinez with me."

"And the reason you're calling is?"

"It's about Petra and Nicolai Mateev."

Roman was silent for a moment. "You have my attention, brother."

Ian gave a quick rundown of the facts as he knew them, ending with his best guess as to why all this was happening. "I think Petra arrived at Joe Owens's as he was being attacked by Albright, the doctor. Albright and Petra are friends and he knew about her migraines and that she could lose consciousness. He framed her for the crime—and maybe even killed Joe, who was supposed to recover. And now he has to get rid of Petra."

"It makes sense," said Roman, "But where does Mateev fit into all of this?"

"My best guess? It was Mateev's raw drugs, and

then money was laundered through Arnie Hatch and his companies."

As he spoke, Ian knew it wasn't simply a guess. He was right. And now the rich and powerful were trying to silence anyone who knew their dirty secrets. He added, "I need you to get in touch with Jones. Tell him what we told you."

"Call him yourself," Roman said. "He'll want to hear from you directly."

"I'm going after her, Roman. I can't let her die without doing everything in my power to save her."

"I would tell you to wait. We can have a SWAT team and helicopters to you within the hour. Hell, we can even get a tank. But I know you won't wait."

"No," said Ian. "I won't."

"I've always got your back," said Roman.

Ian paused. There was so much he wanted to say. But there it was again, the ticking clock urging him on, every second taking him further away from his objective—saving Petra. But at least if he died now, Roman would know—and know why.

"Same to you," he said, and ended the call.

Ian put the auto in gear and pulled back onto the road. He dropped his foot on the accelerator. In less than a minute, the hood was pointed at the closed gate of the industrial park. The tires chewed up the dirt road and spat it behind them in a cloud of dust. Ian crouched low in the seat, tense and ready for incoming bullets.

There was nothing, not even a single shot fired.

He pushed his foot harder on the accelerator. The

speedometer climbed. Seventy miles per hour. Eighty. Ninety. He hit the fence as the gauge reached a hundred. The gate flew open, then snapped back after the SUV shot through.

It hadn't been locked.

Ian took his foot off the gas and let the car idle.

"That was easy," said Martinez.

He agreed. "It was. I don't like it. They could be drawing us into a trap."

"Or maybe Mateev isn't here at all."

"Both of those options are awful. But we've come too far to turn back now." Ian pulled his tablet computer from between the seats and found the beacon for Petra's location. "It's the second warehouse on the left."

He drove to the front door and turned off the ignition. The silence was total. Ian felt a target on his forehead and at the same time, the complete absence of another soul for miles—save for Martinez.

They exited the SUV. It felt as if they'd stepped into an oven. An eagle flew overhead, its wings outstretched as it dipped and rose on the thermals. They hadn't discussed a tactical approach, but Martinez had dropped down behind the quarter panel, his gun aimed at the door, ready to provide backup.

Ian, gun arm outstretched, ran to the building. He pressed his back to the wall. Despite his clothes, the corrugated metal scorched his skin. If there were people in the building, Ian's arrival was hardly a surprise. Still, he wouldn't do Petra any good if he got shot.

Maintaining his vigilance, he pushed the door

open. His world shrank, becoming one hand on the door and the other on his weapon. He dropped to his knee and pivoted. Pebbles tore the fabric of his jeans and the skin beneath. A wedge of light fell into the darkened room, but even from where he knelt, Ian saw it was empty—save for a red car.

He recognized it at once as the sedan Albright had driven to the football stadium. Caring nothing for caution, Ian rose to his feet and sprinted to the passenger window.

She wasn't there. He tried the door handle. It opened.

After holstering his gun, Ian dived across the seats for the automatic trunk release. His hand slipped from the seat to the floor.

There, he felt it. He knew it was hers the moment his fingers brushed the smooth metal.

With shaking hands, he picked it up and stood.

Martinez was at his back. With his firearm still out, he scanned the room for threats. "What is it?" he asked.

Ian held it up. "We found the phone, but not Petra."

Keeping low, Petra crept toward the next metal drum. The hard floor bit into her knees and scraped her palms, but she ignored the pain, focusing only on escaping.

"You," said Mateev. "Check the monitors and see if she made it to the front door. You two take flashlights and find her."

"Me?" Petra recognized Rick Albright's voice.

"Yes, you," said Mateev in answer to the question. "You're the one who decided to frame her for Joe's murder, so you're the one who has the most to lose."

She cursed silently. Rick had used their friendship against her. And now he was hunting her—like he would a wild animal. A fire began in her middle, spreading upward, changing her fear to anger.

Twin beams of light started dancing across the floor. She got to her feet and sprinted the last few yards. The soles of her shoes slapped against the concrete. A beam of light blinded her just as she dived behind a tower of drums.

"There she is," Rick shouted. "Over there."

Light shone from around the sides of the drum, illuminating the floor. The drums hadn't been stacked as closely as Petra had originally thought. They were set in a haphazard maze that wound to who knew where.

Footfalls pounded on the floor as three men approached. She didn't have time to think of a plan, only move. On her feet again, she dashed behind another tower, darting and running without any destination in mind.

Time no longer held meaning and Petra didn't know how far she'd run, nor how long, when she finally paused behind a drum. Crouching low, she looked and listened. The beams from the flashlights were gone, as were the sounds of her pursuers. Yet they hadn't given up—of that she was certain.

With her eyes more accustomed to the dark, Petra

found three towers set together to form a darkened alcove. She slipped inside, finally safe, and waited.

Her heart pounded out the seconds. One. Two. Three. In less than a minute, a shadowy figure moved past.

"Petra," Rick whispered. "I know you're around here somewhere. I'm not going to take you to Mateev, but you have to come out, so we can talk."

Did he really know that she was nearby? If he did, then Petra had found the worst place to hide—in a cell of her own making.

"Petra." Rick's shadow stretched across the floor.

He had doubled back and paced in front of where she now hid. He had seen her come this way; she was now sure of it. At the same time, he didn't know exactly where she was hiding. Now she really was trapped. She stepped farther into the shadows.

"Petra," he said again. "I'm sorry for all of this, really. I didn't mean for anything to happen—not to you, not to Joe. I've gotten myself in too deep with these guys and they're dangerous. But if we work together, maybe we can both escape." Rick stopped pacing and exhaled. He stood in an alleyway between the rows of metal containers. His shoulders were stooped, and he shook his head.

Should she trust him? She wanted to. At one time, he had been her friend. And now? She wanted to share the burden of escape with someone else. But then she thought of Joe.

Rick had been his friend, too. He'd been his physician. Joe had trusted him. And now Joe was dead.

As if Rick could read her mind, he began to speak again. "I was working on a painkiller—that's how it started. But the drugs I used actually did more than help with pain, they made the athletes stronger and faster. Joe tried them, and they worked—he was unstoppable in the Super Bowl, you remember."

Remember. The one word brought it all back. Petra was in Joe's hallway, her head pounding and her vision blurry. There was a footstep behind her, she began to turn and sharp pain split her skull. She heard the thwack of something hitting her head. She felt the reverberation in her teeth. Toppling forward, she hit the ground.

Then there was nothing, until her wrist hurt. Her arm was stretched out and she opened her eyes and looked up. It was Rick, sweating and bloodied, dragging her down the hall. Relief washed over her as the last of her memories returned. Yet it was a hollow victory. Her life was still in jeopardy.

Rick sighed, like a man with regrets. Too bad that Petra had no sympathy.

"Like with all medication, there are side effects," he said, continuing his confession. "They made Joe angry and he couldn't concentrate. He wanted to stop taking them and let the world know what the meds did. But he'd already ruined his life. He didn't need to ruin mine. We fought." Rick's voice broke. "It became physical and I was taking a pretty good beating. I think he would've killed me if I hadn't stopped him. What I did was self-defense, but I never meant to hurt him. I never meant to involve you."

The whole scenario became clear to Petra. She understood that while Rick's car wreck was real, it had also been his orchestration to give him a reason for his injuries. Most likely, he'd waited until he saw someone texting and driving, then purposefully hit them. What was the other driver to say about the crash?

"What about last night?" she asked. Her voice echoed in the cavernous space and Rick spun in a quick circle.

"What about it?"

"You tried to kill me in my own apartment."

He slowly turned toward her hiding place. He looked into the darkness, his eyes narrowed. He knew where she was. She tensed, bracing for the attack. It didn't come.

"I didn't go there to kill you," he said. "I'd taken a set of glasses from Joe's. One was mine, the other his. I wanted to plant his glass at your apartment. The physical evidence would be insurance for me in case you remembered anything."

The throbbing in her head amplified, pounding harder with each beat of her heart. But she couldn't give in. She had to escape. After crouching down, like a runner in the starting blocks, Petra launched herself at Rick. She wrapped her arms around his knees, tackling him the way she'd seen players do on the gridiron.

They both tumbled to the side, hitting a metal drum with a clang that echoed in the cavernous warehouse. She let go of Rick as he toppled to the ground.

Looking up, she found the closest window and began to run.

A crack, like the snapping of a whip, came from behind and a spark hit the drum next to her head. A slug ricocheted off the metal before lodging into the floor. She snapped her head around in time to see Rick. With the gun aimed at her head, he pulled the trigger a second time.

Chapter 15

"This way," one of the Russians called. "The gunfire's over there."

Petra didn't bother to see who found her first. She kept her eyes on the windows—her only point of reference—and ran, weaving in and out among the drums and cans. Then she was there, at the wall. She looked left and right, silently cursing. There was no door—not here at least. Keeping her hand on the wall, Petra began to run again. Ahead, a seam of sunlight shone on the floor. A door.

Arms pumping, legs driving, heart racing, she ran. Her fingers connected with a handle and she pulled it open. Bright sunlight streamed into the room and she took another step forward. A figure emerged from the shadows and grabbed her around the waist, pulling her hard and driving all the air from her lungs. She was lifted from the ground, her feet dangling.

Terror gripped Petra's chest with an icy hand, stilling her heart. Her mind stuttered. She couldn't think, couldn't plan, couldn't react.

"Stupid woman," he said. His breath smelled of cheap vodka and cigarettes. Even though he was at her back, she could tell that he was tall—towering over her at six foot five or maybe more. His chest was solid and his arms were large and powerful, making him an impossible enemy for her to defeat physically.

"You really thought that you could just sneak away?" he asked. "Why did you not realize that the door would be the first place to set up an ambush?"

She hadn't been thinking—that was the problem—only trying to escape. But now that the Russian had her, she wasn't about to remain an easy victim. Petra jabbed back with her elbow, striking her captor in his solar plexus.

The Russian cursed. "Do not make this harder on yourself." He shook her with each word. She flopped in the large man's grasp, then bent double and bit the other hand that held her.

The man screamed and dropped her to the floor. To her left, the cans had been stacked in stair steps, giving her one way to escape—up. She hefted herself onto a drum, finding the top greasy and slick. The stench of oil hung thick in the air.

The Russian grabbed her foot and she kicked him in the face. He fell back to the floor. She climbed to the next drum and the one after that. Her attacker was on his feet again, climbing after her.

Petra ended at the top, with no place else to go, and still the Russian pursued her. She kicked the lower drum. It rocked forward and settled back in place. She braced her back on the wall and placed her feet on the lip of the drum. With all her strength, she straightened her legs. The barrel slowly pitched forward and then gravity took over.

The big Russian looked up, his eyes wide. Then he was gone, his screams lost in the clatter of metal on metal. The drum lay on the floor, a hole in the side leaking thick black oil. It rocked, hitting the crushed body of the big Russian, before rolling out and then back in again. He lay without moving, breathing, his lifeless gaze staring at nothing.

Fumes rose in the air. Petra gagged and wiped her watering eyes.

"Stop right there," said Rick. He had found her. He stood on the floor with his gun in his hand. Feet braced, he aimed the pistol.

Without any place to hide, Petra slowly lifted her hands. The other Russian came up from behind at a jog. He looked at his fallen comrade and then at Petra, his eyes narrowed. Her heart skipped a beat as she wondered what kind of revenge he would extract for the death of his friend.

Rick moved his finger to the trigger. He pulled. A spark erupted from the barrel of the gun. The bullet tore a hole through the metal wall behind her at the same moment that a ball of fire exploded from the floor.

* * *

Ian and Martinez stood at the empty trunk of Rick's rental car.

For Ian, this was the worst-case scenario. The single lead had brought him to a dead end. He opened Petra's phone. His contact information was on the screen. Ian's throat closed and his heart seized. It was the same feeling he'd had when Travis died all those years ago. The implosion of emotion, where all the hurt and anger and sadness comingled into a dense mass, a black hole of feelings.

Ian had lost himself in that void, struggling out only when he met Petra. And if she were gone, truly gone, how would he find the light again?

"What's next, General?" Martinez asked.

Ian hadn't a clue. He had no place to look or any other way to find her. Yet he needed to make a decision.

Before he could, a blast rattled the windows and the ground shook, choking off whatever he might have said. "What was that?"

"It felt like an earthquake, but that's impossible."

The acerbic smell of smoke filled the air. "I think it was an explosion," said Ian.

He raced for the door. Smoke billowed from another warehouse—the one farthest from the gate. It was Petra, of that he was certain. The question now was, had she survived the explosion? Or even after all this, was she truly gone?

Nikolai Mateev stood next to his bed and stared at the bank of monitors. The closed-circuit TVs were the only security for this out-of-the-way and forgotten location. That and his bodyguards. Mateev's blood went cold and his bowels cramped. He stared at a live picture of the open gate and a heavily pixelated SUV.

It was Ian Wallace. He had found Nikolai, after all.

"Ilya," he yelled. "Anatoly."

There was no answer. Everyone was gone. They were looking for Petra Sloane, the same woman Ian Wallace had come to find.

The floor shook suddenly, sending Nikolai off balance. He held on to the bed and waited for the shaking to stop. A funnel of fire shot up at the far side of the warehouse. Fingers of flame danced along the ceiling before burning themselves out.

Metal, scorched and black, remained. The air heated as a fire at the far side of the warehouse raged. There was enough distance that Nikolai wasn't immediately concerned. And yet if his sense of direction was right—and it was—the blast had happened near the only door to the warehouse. And thousands of gallons of highly flammable oil blocked his path to the exit.

Flames shot up around Petra, trapping her and cloaking her in a thick cloud of smoke. Her eyes burned and watered. Her lungs were raw and hurt with each breath. Coughing and choking, she dropped to her knees. Instinct drove her from the flames and she crawled atop the wall of drums. All the while, she knew that she was taking herself farther into the warehouse and away from the only exit.

The smoke lessened as the flames were fed by the fresh air and drawn toward the door. The cloud dissipated, and Petra could both breathe and see. She took a moment to take stock of her location.

Obviously, stuck atop containers of flammables in the midst of a fire was the worst place to be. Three rows over, Petra saw what she needed. She leaped from one tower to the next and then to the one beyond. The next stack of drums was only three high, and she carefully lowered herself down a level. Then to a stack of drums only two high. She turned and gripped the lid of one, then dropped the last few feet to the floor.

"We finally meet."

The voice came from behind Petra, but she didn't need to turn around to know who had spoken. It was undoubtedly Nikolai Mateev.

"Put your hands up where I can see them and turn to face me."

Petra hated having to obey the Russian criminal, yet she wasn't willing to die simply to be spiteful. Lifting her arms, she slowly complied.

Petra had seen Mateev before—when he'd attacked her at the apartment, and then today, as she lay on the floor, pretending to be unconscious. But standing face-to-face, she was finally able to get a sense of who she was up against.

Mateev was a large man, both tall and broad. Wisps of white hair covered his scalp and his jowls sagged. His skin was slightly yellowed. His lips were chapped and cracked. In her estimation, Mateev was both old and infirm. But he was far from harmless.

It was his eyes. He watched her with dispassion and at the same time cunning. It was as if Petra were a bug in a jar that Mateev planned to dissect just because he could.

Ian dropped his foot on the accelerator and turned the steering wheel. The warehouse came into view. A large door was open. Fire licked around the frame and a cloud of black smoke rolled out along the ground. Even in the car, he could feel the inferno's heat push him back. An acrid chemical odor filled the air.

Martinez sat in the seat beside him. He held a phone at his ear and spoke. "There's a fire, possibly chemical, at the industrial park owned by Hatch Enterprises. We need help and backup, STAT."

Two figures, hunched over, emerged from a cloud of smoke and flames. Was one of them Petra? Ian strained to see any distinguishing features—hair, clothes, face. The two were nothing more than dark forms in a fog of billowing soot. Ian dropped his foot all the way down, pressing the accelerator to the floor and sending the SUV flying forward. Then he stepped on the brake and skidded sideways to a stop.

Throwing the door open, he hit the ground at a sprint. He wasn't the praying type, not really believing in anything more than his own strength of will. As he ran toward what was surely the gateway to hell, he hoped a higher power had been watching out for Petra and allowed her to escape the inferno.

Ian got closer and pulled up short. The figures were men: One was Albright. Ian didn't know the other.

Martinez was just a step behind Ian, his gun out and at the ready. "Hold it right there," the detective said. "Lift your hands where I can see them."

Neither man complied, but they were hardly a threat. Both dropped to their knees, coughing and retching.

Ian grabbed Albright by the collar and hefted him to his feet. The doctor's face was blackened with soot, his eyes red and watery. Ian had no sympathy for the man's plight, nor joy for what he had survived.

"Where is she?" Ian asked. "Where's Petra?"

Albright lifted a hand and pointed to the warehouse. "She's in there." His voice was nothing more than a wheeze. "But you'll never find her. The whole place is filled with drums of used motor oil. It's a bomb waiting to explode."

Ian let go and the doctor fell to the ground.

Martinez kept his gun trained on Albright and the other man. "The fire department is on its way. They'll be here in five minutes, maybe ten."

"Petra doesn't have five minutes to live," said Ian. In reality, he wasn't sure she'd survive the next five seconds. But he had no other options. "I'm going in."

"Are you crazy?" cried Martinez. "You can't do that. I won't let you."

"Shoot me if you want, but short of a bullet to my brain, I'm going to find Petra."

Ian cast a glance over his shoulder. In the distance,

a line of SUVs approached the industrial park. It was the RMJ team. Roman must've called them together. Why had Ian ever shut them out of this—the most important investigation of his life?

Roman, Cody, Julia—hell, even Jones. They were the family he was looking for.

"Is that your crew?" the detective asked.

Ian nodded. "Tell them," he said to Martinez. There were no words for Ian's feelings. "Tell them I said thanks."

He looked again to the warehouse and the flames.

"Your gun," said Martinez. "Give it to me—otherwise you'll blow a hole in your chest."

Martinez was right—gunpowder and flames made a deadly combination. And yet, without his Walther, Ian would be unarmed. Already he was thinking about what he needed to do to be successful. But no gun was better than being foolishly dead. Taking the Walther from the holster, he pressed it into Martinez's free hand.

Then he turned back to the warehouse, and ducking to avoid the flames, ran inside.

Nikolai Mateev had nothing to lose. Either way, he was a dead man. Would it be the cancer that finally corrupted his insides, so that he was filled with nothing more than sludge? Or would he die in this fiery warehouse? He preferred a comfortable bed and plenty of morphine to being roasted alive—who wouldn't? But there was one place he refused to perish and that was in prison.

Motioning with the gun, Nikolai directed the woman away from the drums of oil and her back to the bed and the table filled with monitors. The computer screens were all black, the wires most likely burned by the encroaching fire. But the hanging bulb still worked, and for the moment, they had light.

Nikolai sat on the edge of the bed. His legs hurt and the gun in his hand was too heavy. He ignored the discomfort and said, "We wait for your boyfriend, Ian Wallace, to save you. Then he'll save us both."

The woman's long dark hair clung to her sweaty cheeks and neck. Her face was flushed and the flames behind her danced and undulated, throwing their shadows across Petra's body. He knew exactly what had attracted Ian Wallace to her. It was more than her beauty; it was her strength, as well. That was evident in the set of her jaw and her unwavering glare.

"You're delusional," she said.

He ignored her comment. He needed her alive. "I've known your man a long time, you know."

"You don't know Ian. You're a criminal he's been chasing."

"I am a business man, but there was a time when I wanted to recreate the world order."

She spat on the floor. "You? A revolutionary?"

Beautiful, strong and spunky. It was quite an intoxicating mixture. "Why do you think that at one time I didn't want to change the world?"

Petra looked away. He didn't blame her. In these last few months, Nikolai had become maudlin.

"The corruption in Russia was enough to make

a man sick," he continued. "And the West, with all their talk of freedom and liberty and justice? It was just talk. That's when I got the idea of making war. I found others willing to work with me. One of them was a physicist and we made a bomb meant for London. It wouldn't have killed many, but enough. Then, when the West investigated, they wouldn't see a group of rogue attackers, but Russians."

"And the ensuing counterattack would get rid of the corrupt leaders?"

That's exactly what he had wanted. "And you're smart, too."

"And you failed, obviously."

"It was Ian Wallace who found me. He got the bomb and I escaped."

"And you became a criminal who doesn't care about anyone other than yourself."

"Not true," said Nikolai. But it was.

"What changed?" she asked.

"I became pragmatic."

"Then why are we here, roasting to death?"

"We are waiting for Ian Wallace, like I said."

"He probably has no idea where I am, and he certainly wouldn't know how to find me."

"That's where you're wrong," said Nikolai. "He's here, now."

"Ian's here?" she whispered, her eyes bright.

Never had anyone looked at him with such hope as Petra held for Ian Wallace.

Nikolai had seen desperation many times. Greed?

Respect? Of course. He'd even seen lust, but underneath it all was fear.

But hope? Never. In that moment, Nikolai truly hated the Brit.

"Why are we here?" she asked. "What do you really want?"

"I want to go back to Russia. Ian won't let me simply walk away. But to save you, I imagine he'll do just about anything—including letting me go."

"So I'm your hostage?"

"Only until I get back to Russia."

Petra shook her head. "Ian would never go for that. He's been after you for over ten years. You're crazy."

Nikolai shrugged. A certain amount of insanity had kept him alive all these years. The air was hot; it dried his lungs. Sweat dripped down the side of his face. He wiped it away. "Not much longer now," he said.

"What if you have this all wrong?" Petra asked. "What if Ian doesn't try to save me?"

"I've seen Ian Wallace confront death to save a stranger before. Imagine what he would do for someone he loves?"

Petra turned and gestured to the wall of flames that separated them from the exit, keeping out anyone who might try and save them. "What if he tries, but can't reach us?"

She had a point, he'd give her that.

Still… "I am prepared to die," said Nikolai.

A bit of ash floated by, looking to him like a blackened snowflake. Would he ever feel the icy kiss of a Russian winter again? In truth, he thought not.

"And if I should die here?" He laughed bitterly. "Well, I'll only have to spend one minute longer in hell."

Chapter 16

A towering inferno loomed over Ian. His eyes watered. His lungs squeezed every time he took a breath. Each exhalation racked his body with a cough that bent him double. Smoke hung thick in the air, blinding him and confusing his sense of direction, until he no longer knew where he was.

More than that, Ian had no idea how long he'd been wandering in the fire. Seconds? Minutes? To him, it felt like days. Without a way to gauge his progress, he had no other choice than to move on.

He pulled the side of his jacket over his head and raced forward. With his heart pounding, he felt flames lick at his skin. A crack, like a gunshot, came at him from behind. He turned in time to see the lid of an oil drum, spinning like the devil's discus, come directly at his head. Ian spun to the right just as the cover slammed into another barrel. Sparks exploded and bits of hot ash caught him on the neck.

He looked for a place to go, a space to inhabit that would help him survive for one more minute.

Survive. The word hit him like a bullet to the gut. How could Petra survive in this inferno? And if she was alive now, how would he ever reach her? Ian drew a breath and it came without pain. The smoke had lessened. He wiped a sooty hand down his face and found that the worst of the flames was behind him. More than that, he heard noises.

Then he realized they were voices, and he strained to listen. One was deep and slow—a male voice. The other was higher and soft. From the cadence and intonations, Ian knew that he'd found Petra—and most likely Nikolai Mateev.

He followed the sounds and, as he knew he would, he found them—Nikolai and Petra. She stood with her back to where Ian hid. Nikolai sat on a hospital bed, a gun in his hand, pointed at her.

Ian didn't take time to congratulate himself or thank his lucky stars for finding Petra alive and well. Instead, he assessed the situation—and really, it was all crap. Nikolai Mateev was the only one with a firearm. Ian first had to reach Petra and then get her away. If both those things happened—without either of them getting shot—they were still in the middle of a burning building.

And then it all became painfully simple. His plan

of attack had a single focus: save Petra, no matter the cost.

Ian stepped from his hiding place, hands lifted. "Nikolai," he called out.

The Russian lifted his eyes and squinted into the fire. "Amusing, is it not?" said Mateev. "That after all these years we finally meet, face-to-face."

Ian found no humor in the situation. "We can get to know each other better later," he said. "Let Petra go. She can hardly be important to you."

"That's where you are mistaken." Nikolai stared at Ian, and their eyes locked—neither one willing to look away.

In the briefest instant, all those years faded and Ian was once again on the damp platform of the London Tube. Mateev's hand was on the homeless man's shoulder. They had stared at each other in that moment, too. Then Nikolai had pushed the man onto the tracks and Ian had a choice to make.

For more than a decade and a half, he had studied Mateev, and was now as familiar with him as he was his own shadow. Was that his gambit now? To use Petra as the latest gaming piece for another escape?

And then Ian was back inside the warehouse, nothing more than an oven already roasting them alive. He didn't have time to play games and he cut to the chase. "Petra? Are you okay?"

Her eyes were moist and shiny as she nodded. Ian wanted nothing more than to hold her and tell her that it would all turn out fine. But what if that was a lie? "What do you want, Mateev?"

"I want to go to Russia and I want the doctor, Albright, to come with me."

Mateev's first demand made sense. Hell, Ian wasn't even surprised. But the doctor? "Albright?"

"If he still lives, he comes with me," said the Russian.

"Albright, that piece of crap—he made it out. But I have to ask, why do you want him?"

"He provides me with treatments. He is useful to me. You will get me out of this fire and let me go free. I have a jet waiting at a local airport and it will be allowed to take off. Once my party has landed safely in Moscow, I will have Petra delivered to the United States embassy. Those are my terms and there will be no negotiation. If you don't agree, I'll shoot the woman and then myself. I will not be taken to jail."

Ian wanted to ask if Mateev had cancer and if the treatments given by Albright had something to do with that illness. He stopped himself. The why of the situation mattered little.

"You have a deal," said Ian.

"No," Petra gasped. "Ian, you can't."

He stepped forward. Nikolai got to his feet with more speed than Ian would have guessed. The old Russian grabbed Petra by the arm, pulling her to him and pressing the gun to her side.

Ian didn't bother to question whether Mateev was sincere. He was a sick man with nothing to lose. "You have my word," Ian said. "You will get back to Russia, unharmed."

"And the doctor?"

Albright. Ian wanted to roar. "Him, too."

"That's what I thought. Now, get us out of here."

Ian pivoted where he stood, trying to find the path he had taken, but it was gone. A wall of fire marched forward. Saint and sinner, it didn't matter—foot by foot, hell was coming to claim them all.

Mateev had Petra by the arm. The gun bit into her ribs, bruising her flesh. She didn't care. How could Ian let Nikolai Mateev just walk away? But she knew better than to ask. It was for her—Ian was doing all of it to save her life. She silently cursed her stupidity for trusting Rick Albright.

"Don't let him go, Ian," she said, pulling away.

Mateev's grip tightened. "Stop struggling," the old man hissed.

But why should she listen? He wasn't going to shoot her. She was his only way out of the warehouse and back to Russia. If she could get away from him, he would have nothing.

It gave her an idea—an absolutely insane idea that just might work.

She jabbed her elbow hard into Mateev's middle. He wheezed, his hold loosening. Bringing Mateev's shoulder back and his elbow at an angle, she twisted and ran.

Petra bolted forward—toward the flames. They rose in the air, orange and black, mesmerizing and deadly. The heat enveloped her. Each breath burned her nose and dried her lungs.

Nikolai was right behind her, chasing her, the gun

in his hand. *"Ostanovites ili ya budu strelyat,"* he shouted.

She didn't need to know Russian to understand what he meant: *get back here, or you'll get shot.*

Petra had no intention of stopping, any more than he planned to shoot. But she was heartened to hear that he still had his gun. All she needed was the right moment...

Petra pushed on each drum as she passed, with Nikolai close behind. They were all filled and heavy. And then she found it, a drum of oil that was set apart from the rest, that rocked when she pushed on the rim. She raced to the far side and shouldered the container over. It hit the floor with a crash and oil spilled out in a wave.

Nikolai was too close to stop. The oil splashed upon him, soaking his clothes. He lost his footing and slipped, holding on to the floor to gain purchase and move forward. Nikolai Mateev stood upright. Oil dripped from his hands and the gun he still held. It stained his knees and turned his face black and greasy.

"You're a stupid cow," the old man snarled. "You want to kill me? Well, now we can both die." He lifted his gun and took aim.

Nikolai had the woman in his sights. Petra Sloane had proved to be a bothersome creature and he felt no remorse that she would perish at his hand. His finger moved to the trigger. He applied the slightest pressure.

A blur came in from Nikolai's periphery, knocking him sideways as the gun fired, the recoil jerking the weapon from his hand. As he went over, he saw the woman dodge behind an oil drum.

Before he could take aim a second time, Nikolai was flat on his back. Ian Wallace straddled him, his weight crushing Nikolai's chest. It forced the air from his lungs and prevented him from drawing a breath.

Yet even as he lay prone beneath his nemesis, he felt the effects of Albright's treatment finally kicking in, the strength beginning to course into his body. He lifted his hips and hooked his legs over Wallace's shoulders, pulling the other man back, flattening him to the ground. He drove his fist into Ian's face. Blood erupted from the Brit's mouth and Nikolai's knuckles throbbed from the impact.

It felt good to hurt. It felt better to cause pain.

Years of indignation at being hunted and chased filled Nikolai with power. He drew back his arm again, focusing all his strength on Ian's nose. With as much ferocity as he could muster, he swung his fist once more.

Ian shifted to the right in the last instant. Nikolai missed the Brit's face by a millimeter, his fist slamming into the floor. Bone connected with concrete. Pain shot through his knuckles and radiated all the way to his shoulder. His stomach threatened to revolt.

Then Ian was on his feet.

The gun was there; Nikolai saw it, just to his left. He scrambled for the weapon, sliding on the oily floor. His fingers found the grip and he rolled to his back and fired. The Brit recoiled and tensed at the noise and the flash, his expression shocked as he realized that he had not been hit.

Slowly, Ian looked over his shoulder. Even from where Nikolai was sprawled on the floor, he could see the wound's black-red bloom open and spread across Petra Sloane's shoulder. Her eyes were wide, a silent scream on her lips. She collapsed on the floor and Nikolai smiled.

And then he was in agony. His hand exploded with pain as a blue flame crept from the barrel of the gun to the slide, to the grip, to his wrist. It consumed his exposed hand. He dropped the fiery gun and brushed the flames away. They refused to be extinguished.

Fire spread up his arms, across his chest and around his back. It spread beyond his neck to his face, his eyes, his scalp. And it spread. And spread, until there was no place left for the fire to go and nothing left to burn.

An invisible fist punched Petra and knocked her to the floor. White heat bored a hole through her shoulder. She tried to push off the floor, but her arm refused to hold her and she fell back.

Ian was at her side. His fingers dug painfully into her shoulder. "Just lie still," he said, "and breathe."

"That old bastard shot me," she said, gasping for air. Petra tried to sit up. "I'm bleeding."

"I know, love," he said. "If we don't keep pressure on this wound you'll bleed out. Just lie still."

A scream came from above. But it wasn't a sound

made by a human. It was industrial, metallic—as the roof bent and bowed. She grabbed Ian's wrist and pulled his hand from her shoulder. "Go," she said. "This place is going to collapse any second. You can't save me and I don't want you to die trying."

"If you think I'm leaving you here, you're crazy."

Tears collected in her lashes. "Ian, I love you. I always have and I always will. Let me go and save yourself."

"Petra." His voice was hoarse. "Don't talk like that." He reached for her hand and placed it on her shoulder. He squeezed her knuckles hard. "Hold this wound as tight as you can. Do you hear me?"

She did, but his voice sounded as if it came from far away. She held her shoulder, and her hand filled with hot blood. Her muscles grew fatigued and her grip loosened. Her eyelids felt heavy.

"Petra!" Hearing her name roused her. Ian was still at her side, although, inexplicably, he was shirtless. "I've made a bandage out of my shirt." He slid the bandage under her hand. He said, "Don't move, but stay awake, Petra. You've been shot and are in shock. If you pass out, you might not wake up. Do you hear me?"

She tried to speak. The words wouldn't come.

Ian touched her face. "Petra. Stay awake."

She could comprehend only one word. *Awake.*

"Good," he said. And then Ian was gone.

She forced her eyes to remain open, despite the fact that they wanted to close of her own accord. Yet Ian's dire warning about falling asleep and not waking again stayed with her. She needed to focus on something, anything, yet nothing came to mind. "Awake," she said out loud. "Awake. Awake. Awake…"

She was too tired to speak and her words trailed off. Maybe if she closed her eyes for only a moment, it wouldn't be so bad.

The roof overhead groaned as the structure weakened. Ian had to get them out of the warehouse, and fast. Worse than the ceiling threatening to collapse, Petra had lost too much blood and needed immediate medical treatment.

And that wasn't even the worst of it. The fire still raged and was creeping closer with every passing second. The lightbulb above his head flickered once and then exploded, scattering bits of glass on the floor.

With nothing more than the high windows above for light now, the flames looked brighter, closer, larger. The windows… Ian looked up. More than thirty feet from the warehouse floor, the windows were their only hope of escaping.

Ian devised a crude plan, improvising with what was on hand. He pushed the hospital bed next to the wall. Next, he retrieved the table that had held the monitors. Leaning it against the wall, he folded the legs in place so they faced out, like rungs of a rickety ladder. Finally, he gathered up fifteen yards of wiring that had been used for the closed-circuit TVs and fashioned a harness.

He knelt next to Petra. Her skin was pale, and even in the orange-and-red firelight, Ian could tell that her lips were turning blue. Her eyes were opened to slits. Her mouth moved, but no sound came out. He wasn't even sure if she could hear him as he shared his crazy-ass plan. "I'm going to carry you and climb to the top of that table. From there, I'll break through the window and then we can rappel down. Got that?"

She didn't answer. Scooping up Petra, Ian couldn't, and wouldn't, think about what would come later.

With Petra in his arms and the cable looped over his shoulder, Ian used the table as a makeshift ladder. At the top, he inspected the window. The glass was single paned, but thick. He'd hoped for a latch or a slide that opened it. There was neither.

What he did have was an industrial plug on the end of the cable. If enough force was applied, it could be used to break the glass. Yet hammering through the pane was only the beginning of his problems. Ian would need to keep his balance, while holding a seriously injured person.

His options were limited. Grasping the plug, Ian struck the glass with it.

Nothing happened. He hit it again, then again. Jostled by the action, Petra cried out in pain. At least she was still conscious, but how much more could she tolerate before passing out?

Bracing his legs to balance atop the table, Ian threw a side punch that began in his back and gained power with every inch it traveled from shoulder to arm to wrist to hand. The glass splintered but didn't shatter.

Ian cursed. After drawing back again, he swung

the plug hard on the window. Cracks spread in all directions and a hole broke in the glass.

"Ian," Petra said, her voice little more than a whisper. "Look out. Above you."

He turned as a coil of flame, blue and orange, raced across the ceiling, drawn to the fresh air. He cradled Petra to his chest and jumped down, hitting the bed before bouncing to the floor. A haze of smoke and ash surrounded them as the whole ceiling became awash in flames.

A screeching sound, like auto brakes gone bad, filled the warehouse. A single shard of glass rocketed to the bed, the sharp end impaling the mattress. Another piece fell and then another. But at least the window was open.

The fire receded as quickly as it came. He had only a minute to get them out before the flames would return, only this time they wouldn't burn out so quickly. He scrambled up onto the bed, then climbed the legs of the table. At the top, he worked the harness over Petra's hips and waist, pulling the cords taut. He tied one end to an exposed beam of steel in the window's casing. Wrapping the ends around his hands, he pressed his feet to the wall and walked up and over the windowsill.

The whole building undulated. Ian clamped Petra to his chest. "Hold on," he said. "We have just one shot at this."

With one hand grasping the cords, the other gripping Petra tight, Ian pressed his feet to the steel siding and began to walk down. The wall bowed inward from the pressure. Sparks rose from the roof. Ian loosened his grip on the cords and let them slide. The plastic coating burned his palm, but he didn't care.

With five feet left, he dropped to the dirt. The ground shook. Holding Petra to his chest, Ian ran, though the cord, a black serpent, tried to tether them to the inferno.

He wrestled her from the harness as the metal roof screamed and a pillar of fire rose in the air. Ian dived to the earth, covering Petra's body with his. The roof fell inward and the walls collapsed, the entire building nothing but burned and twisted metal.

The screech of sirens pierced the silent prairie. The road, a tattered black ribbon, was suddenly filled with speeding vehicles and lights and noise. Once again Ian was on his feet, with Petra limp in his arms.

"It's okay," he said as he ran. "It's okay. You're going to be all right."

He met the first ambulance as it arrived on the scene. "She's been shot through the shoulder," he said to the EMT. A stretcher was produced and Petra was laid on it.

Her eyelids fluttered open and then closed. Her lips moved. Ian leaned in close to hear her.

"You made it out of the warehouse," she whispered.

"We made it," he corrected.

She lifted her hand, so cold, to his cheek. He leaned into her palm, her touch the only thing that mattered.

"Excuse me, sir," said an EMT. "I have to start a

saline drip on this patient, so we can stabilize her for transportation. I need her arm."

"I'm going to be right here," said Ian loudly, although he wasn't sure that Petra heard him.

Her eyelids fluttered, and Ian reluctantly let go of Petra's hand. The only thing that could keep him away was saving her life. He stepped to the side, a careful eye on Petra and the EMT's ministrations.

Roman DeMarco came up at a run. He skidded to a stop. "Ian," he said. "Damn, I'm happy to see you. I thought... When the roof collapsed, I thought that you were gone for good. I should've known it'd take more than an inferno to put you in a grave."

Behind them, the fire continued to burn off the last of the oil, the warehouse nothing more than warping metal and a blackened shell. It truly looked like the gateway to hell. "I have no idea how we survived," he muttered.

He looked back at Petra. She was pale, even under all the soot. He bunched his fists, full of rage that he hadn't kept her safe, that in his obsession to find Mateev he'd missed the real person who'd attacked Joe. Rick Albright.

"Ian," said Roman, interrupting his thoughts. "Take this." Roman had stripped out of his flannel shirt, leaving him only in a T-shirt. "You need this more than I do."

"Thanks," said Ian, as he shrugged into the garment. "I used my shirt as a bandage for Petra."

"So, are you going to tell me what happened, or do I have to wait for the debriefing?"

Before Ian could answer, a black SUV with darkened windows pulled up next to the police car. The passenger door opened, and Special Agent Marcus Jones stepped out. Sun glinted off his bald head and reflected in his aviator sunglasses. He smoothed down his tie and looked directly at Ian.

"I guess Jones is going to want to talk to you," said Roman.

"We have to get this patient to the hospital," the EMT said to Ian. "Do you want to ride with her?"

Petra's stretcher had been placed in the back of the ambulance. Without a word, Ian stepped onto the tailgate and slid into a jump seat.

While buckling his five-point harness, Ian leaned over to Roman. "Tell Jones if he wants to talk, he can find me at the hospital."

"But don't you want to wrap up this case?" Roman asked. "I thought bringing down Mateev was your life's purpose."

"I thought so, too," said Ian honestly. "But I was wrong. It's Petra. It's always been her, I was just too damn blind to see."

The EMT slammed the door shut and the ambulance rolled forward, kicking up a cloud of dirt. The world outside the back window disappeared, replaced with a coating of dust.

He didn't care what was happening at the warehouse. He didn't need to be in charge and didn't even worry that there was important intel he would miss.

"Ian?"

He looked at Petra. She regarded him through swollen eyes.

He reached for her hand, wrapping it in both of his. "I'm here," he said. Where she'd felt cold before, her flesh was hot with fever. "Close your eyes and rest now. You're going to the hospital and they'll take care of you."

"It was Rick," she whispered.

"I know," he said. "Rick attacked Joe, framed you and then went back to kill your client."

"I'm innocent."

"I know, love."

"And Nikolai…" She struggled to draw in a breath.

"There's time enough for what happened to Nikolai."

She shook her head slightly. "I heard them talking. I need you to know, in case… Nikolai came here because Rick developed a drug. It was supposed to cure his cancer."

It cleared up a good bit of the mystery, but Ian didn't care. "Just rest," he urged again.

This time Petra nodded. "And, Ian," she said as her eyes drifted closed. "Will you stay with me?"

"Of course," said Ian. "I'm never leaving you again."

Chapter 17

Ian sat in a hospital lounge, waiting for the surgeon's report on Petra. His chest ached and he remembered why he'd stopped wanting to care about anything after Travis Wetherby's death. The pain of loss, he had thought, was worse than the void of apathy. Yet he'd been wrong. The joy in loving someone—and in being loved—was more important than any agony that followed grief.

The question he needed answered was, would Ian only be left with memories of Petra and regret for what might have been? Would *she* be willing to risk a second chance on *him*?

"Care for some company?"

Ian looked to the door. The whole team stood on

the threshold, Roman, Julia, Cody—even Martinez had come along.

"You are all a sight for sore eyes," said Ian as he got to his feet and greeted them.

"How's Petra?" Julia asked.

Ian shrugged. He hated to be uninformed and not able to control the outcome. "She's in surgery. That's all I know."

"So, what happened?" Cody asked. "How'd you two end up in a burning warehouse?"

"Rick Albright kidnapped Petra and took her to Nikolai Mateev, who was hiding out."

"Martinez explained some of what happened to us," Roman said. "But how does a team doctor get involved with Russian gangsters?"

Ian recalled what Petra had told him in the ambulance. "Albright had developed some kind of medicine. My guess is that it started out as something for athletes, but he discovered that it could also be used to treat certain kinds of cancer. And Mateev came to America to seek it out as an experimental treatment."

"And does any of this have to do with Joe Owens?"

Ian hadn't focused on the football star much over the past several hours. The texts to and from Yuri Kuzntov came to mind.

"Joe needed street drugs to counteract a problem, and my guess is that it was the side effects of Albright's meds. When Yuri couldn't supply Joe anymore, he got worse and his behavior declined. Then once the street drugs were out of his system, he started thinking clearly and decided to speak out about the performance enhancer."

"And you think that the doctor figured out what was about to happen," Roman offered. "And then there was a fight that got out of hand?"

It was a possibility, and Ian shrugged. "Or maybe Albright intended to kill Owens from the beginning. In the end, it doesn't matter much."

"That's a lot of maybes and guesses," said Roman.

Ian didn't have anything better than supposition, although he doubted that he was wrong. "Albright will probably confess. He doesn't seem like the type to serve jail time to protect anyone."

"How'd Petra get involved?"

"She is, or rather was, Joe's agent. He called with important news and wanted to meet in person. Petra showed up at Joe's house as the attack was happening. She was just in the wrong place at the wrong time. Albright tried to frame her. It almost worked."

"We have a few updates," said Roman. "Albright and the other man who survived the blaze have been arrested. They've yet to make a statement."

"They will," said Ian. "With Nikolai Mateev dying in that warehouse, there's no more worries about retribution."

Martinez's phone buzzed. He fished it from his pocket and stepped away to answer the call. With shoulders hunched, the cop had his back to the group. He nodded as he spoke, his voice an urgent whisper. He ended the call and cursed before tucking the phone into his jacket.

"Everything okay?" asked Julia.

Martinez pressed his lips together and shook his head. "I gotta get back to my precinct. Word's gotten out in the PD that I never should've been on the Owens case and I shouldn't have been at the warehouse."

"I'm glad you were there," said Ian. "Without you, Albright would've gotten away."

Martinez shrugged. "I'm worried that my job is on the line."

"Oh, Luis," said Julia. "I'm sorry."

"It doesn't matter," said the detective. "Joe was my best friend. He was like a brother. Losing my job is nothing compared to catching his killer."

"Julia," Ian said, "can you take Martinez back to his car? It's parked at my house."

"Sure thing," she said.

Then it was just Ian, along with Cody and Roman. There was a lot that he needed to say to these two men, his operatives. With the three of them working together, they'd brought down the biggest crime syndicate in the world. He owed them something, but his mind was in surgery with Petra.

"I gotta ask," said Roman, thankfully breaking the silence. "You keeping Rocky Mountain Justice closed forever? Was catching Mateev all you needed? Or do you still have more to do?"

"I guess that's it," said Ian. "I don't know. With Petra in surgery, I haven't really thought about it."

"You don't know? That's the biggest shock of all," Roman said. His voice was stern, but his eyes held a heaping dose of skepticism. "You always have a plan for everything."

Ian smiled and gave a laugh. It was cut short by the appearance of the surgeon.

"Mr. Wallace?" The surgeon wore a lab coat over scrubs. His brow was lowered, the corners of his mouth pulled down.

Despite the air-conditioned room, Ian began to sweat. "Yes?"

"Petra Sloane is out of surgery."

"How'd it go?" asked Ian. "How is she?"

"Petra lost a good bit of blood from the bullet wound. Debris from the fire had gotten into the wound and she had already developed an infection. Combined with the amount of smoke she inhaled, she was in acute distress when she arrived."

Ian tightened his jaw to keep from howling with anger. "What does all that mean? How is she?"

"She was in rough shape," he said. "But Ms. Sloane is a tough woman. She'll survive."

Feeling as though a thousand pounds had been lifted from his shoulders, Ian dragged both hands down his face. "Thank you," he said.

Petra was alive, and he intended to keep her with him, always. He just had to convince her that he could go the distance for real.

Petra's throat was raw and her chest burned. Her shoulder throbbed. She opened up her eyes, only to squeeze them shut again. A yellow fluorescent bulb shone behind her head. A continuous beeping filled the quiet.

It took only a moment for her to get her bearing and realize she was in a hospital, which meant that she'd survived being trapped in the burning warehouse and being shot. It also meant that she hadn't blacked out and attacked her client, Joe.

She opened her eyes again, this time slowly. She lay in a typical hospital bed with rails that had various controls. An IV was attached to her arm and clear liquid dripped from a bag that was attached to a pole. A small TV hung on the wall and a newscast played softly. In the corner, Ian slept in a chair.

It was almost hard to believe that he was with her—not wrapping up the Mateev case, his lifelong obsession. Only two years before, he'd let her go so he could continue his hunt for the Russian. Had Ian really changed that much?

It was dark outside, and Petra wondered if Ian had been with her all along. Although she longed to talk to him, and truly find out what she could about the case, it was late. He was tired and if he were asleep, she'd let him rest.

She turned her attention to the TV on the wall. A news anchor sat behind a desk in the studio and looked directly into the camera. "Truly," she said, "this case has rocked the Rocky Mountain state. What began as an assault between athlete and agent has quickly become an international case that involves a drug trafficking ring, murder, kidnapping and athletes being used to test secret drugs."

Petra reached for the remote and considered changing the channel. After all, this was her story and she knew all there was to know. Or did she?

The reporter continued. "The latest bombshell in a story full of explosive twists and turns is the arrest of the Colorado Mustangs' owner, Arnie Hatch." Film showing a handcuffed Hatch being led from the stadium to a waiting police car played as the reporter spoke. "Hatch is accused of working with a known Russian drug lord to develop a performance enhancer that evades detection during NFL drug tests.

"The drugs, developed by team doctor, Richard Albright, had been given to Mustangs quarterback Joe Owens. Owens realized the side effects of the drugs and had decided to go to the authorities. It was then that Albright allegedly attacked Owens and tried to pin the entire incident on Owens's agent, Petra Sloane."

A mug shot of Rick filled the screen. Petra tried to feel angry at him—to find a soul-deep fury for what he'd done and what he'd tried to do. Surprisingly, she didn't feel any anger, only sadness for a good life that had gone bad.

The reporter continued, "Aside from a charge of murder, Albright has been accused of drug trafficking, kidnapping and attempted murder. Even though Albright's attorney said that his client is cooperating fully with police, it's hard to imagine that this doctor will be practicing medicine any time soon."

She used a remote attached to her bed to turn off

the TV. Ian snuffled in his sleep and then sat up, ramrod straight.

"You're awake," he said. He stood and moved to her bedside. "How do you feel?"

"Grateful to be alive. You saved me, Ian. I don't know how to thank you."

"Just keep staying alive and we'll call it even."

Petra gave a small laugh. A pain shot through her shoulder. She winced.

"Do you need anything?" he asked. "Water? Something for the pain?"

She shook her head, suddenly tired again. "Maybe I'll just close my eyes for a minute."

"You go ahead and sleep," he said. "I'll be right here."

Petra had a vague memory of Ian making the same promise in the ambulance. Had he? Or was it just a pleasant dream?

"How long have you been here?" she asked, as she began to sink into sleep.

"I've been here the whole time, Petra. And you aren't getting rid of me. Not this time."

Petra sat on the edge of the hospital bed, her arm in a sling. In their early morning rounds, the doctors had proclaimed her fit enough to be released. She held a stack of discharge papers, the top one a list of dos and don'ts for her recovery. Kat had brought some clothes for Petra—a shirt and pants. And now, Petra was anxious to leave and put this whole episode in her past.

She glanced at the wall clock: 7:32 a.m. She'd spoken to her parents earlier, and they were on their way from Cleveland, expecting to land in Denver by lunch.

All she needed now was Ian.

"Hey," he said. A white bandage was wrapped around his hand, and even though he'd changed clothes—another black T-shirt and jeans—Ian had yet to shower and he still smelled of smoke.

"Hey," she said. She stood, her legs were weak and she stumbled.

Ian was at her side, holding her up. "You need to take it easy." With his arm around her waist, he led her to the door. "You can use this until we get you to the car."

"A wheelchair? I can walk."

"Humor me, then."

She sat. "Humored?"

"Yes. And thank you. It's a media circus outside, just so you know."

Petra groaned.

"Are you going to make a statement?"

With a shake of her head, Petra said, "I never wanted to be famous, much less infamous. I'm better behind the scenes. And besides, I'm not sure what I would say. I just got shot and then ended up here."

Ian began to push the wheelchair down the hall and towards the elevators. He hit the call button and maneuvered the wheelchair into the tiny car. "You did a lot more than just get shot."

"Don't believe everything you see on TV," she teased.

Ian laughed, and the elevator door opened in the lobby.

"Can you at least let me walk out the front door? I'd like to salvage some of my dignity in front of the cable news networks."

"I'm sure that can be arranged," Ian said and he helped her to her feet.

The throng of TV reporters gathered just outside the glass entrance was visible. She inhaled deeply, then exhaled. Holding her head high, she reached for Ian's hand. Together, they walked out the door—ready to face the cameras and the questions.

The lights were blinding. A hundred questions were asked at once. Yet she had Ian at her side. They were a hell of a team and they'd be able to face anything—even the reporters. She recognized one face among the many—her former boss, Mike Dawson.

"How're you doing, kid?" he asked. For a moment, she thought his concern was real. Then she noticed that Mike wasn't looking at her, but rather at the surrounding cameras. He continued, addressing the reporters. "You don't know how worried we've been about you."

"You're right," she said. "I don't know how worried you've been, especially since you fired me because I was accused of—not found guilty of—a horrible crime. Even the justice system presumes innocence."

"Petra, please," Mike said. His brow was damp. He wiped the sweat away with a silk handkerchief. "Let's just be happy that you've been exonerated, and we can discuss everything else at work tomorrow." He turned to the cameras "That's right, you still have your job. What I said the other day was a misunderstanding."

"Let me be plain, then, so we all understand. I quit, Mike."

"Don't be silly, kid. We can work this out."

Silly? "Stop patronizing me. And Mike, you're a jerk."

Mike's mouth hung open. Ian pushed through the crowd of reporters, his grip on Petra's hand never wavering. She followed, never once bothering to look back.

Ian's SUV was parked near the entrance and he opened the passenger door. Petra sank into the seat, thankful that the nightmare was over. She still had questions about what would happen in her life, especially since she'd just quit her job on live TV. And yet there was really only one thing she wanted to know. How did Ian feel about her, about them? Did he want anything at all, or was this truly the end?

Petra was so lost in thought that she didn't realize they'd arrived at Ian's house, and now, well, now she had to make a choice. Her eyes were drawn to the front door.

"It'll be nice to get home," she said. Home. Her condo. That was never her home, just a resting place until… Well, until what?

Until Ian, she supposed.

"You can stay here if you think the press might be waiting for you again," he said.

Petra's heart leaped, but she shook her head. "I'm not sure that it would be wise. Things could get complicated."

"Complicated?" Ian snorted. "I've never seen life more clearly than I do right now. Petra, I love you. I want to be with you. You belong with me. You allow me to feel, and without you, I am a shell of a person."

"Those are nice sentiments, Ian. And honestly, I don't doubt that you love me." She hesitated. "I know I love you."

"Then what's the problem?"

"Us. You don't have a job, you have a calling. And me, I want to matter in a relationship. Neither of us are bad people…" She let her words trail off. "I'm sorry, Ian."

"No," he said. "No way am I going to let you give up on us. On me. I've changed."

"It's not magic. You can't snap your fingers and make everything all better."

Ian worked his jaw back and forth and stared out the window. "When you were shot…when I thought that you might not make it… Damnit, Petra. I thought I knew what was important, but I was wrong. I was stupid and wrong."

"I don't know what to say," she said.

Ian leaned across the dashboard and placed his lips on hers. The kiss was soft and tender. "Just say that you'll come back and that we can try again."

Their relationship wouldn't be flawless, she knew that. Then again, maybe that had been her problem from the beginning. She had expected perfection and not the joy that came from the imperfections of life. And love.

Tears flooded her eyes. "I love you, Ian."

He pressed his forehead to hers. "I love you, too. Let's get you back home."

Hand in hand, they walked to the house. Ian opened the front door. The first chimes of the grandfather clock began to sound as they crossed the threshold. "It's a whole new day," Petra murmured.

"A new day," said Ian. He took her hand in his once more. They fitted together perfectly. "And a new beginning."

Epilogue

August 31
8:00 p.m.

The large rectangular table had been removed from the Rocky Mountain Justice conference room. It was replaced with half a dozen round tables, each covered with a pristine white cloth. The lights were low and candles glowed in the middle of floral centerpieces. Servers clad in tuxedos weaved through the crowd with trays of champagne and tapas. The din of conversation mixed with low tones of the string quartet that played in the corner.

Standing at the door, Ian surveyed the room. This place, and these people, were part of his creation.

Petra moved in next to him and reached for his hand. "Are you ready?" she asked.

Ian's chest was filled with emotion. Excitement for what was next. But no regret for what he was leaving behind. "As long as you're with me." He lifted her hand to his lips and placed a kiss on her soft, smooth skin. "I'm ready for anything."

They were all there—Roman and Madelyn. Cody and Viktoria, along with Viktoria's son, Gregory—who seemed to have grown inches since Ian saw him last. Julia. Katarina and her husband. Even Luis Martinez and Marcus Jones had joined them for the celebration, if for no other reason than it was their victory, as well.

Ian stepped through the door. Conversation stopped and all eyes turned to him.

"My mum always said that if you approach and all chatter stops, be worried—be very, very worried." He gave a wry smile. "And right now, you all have me terrified."

His remark was met with polite laughter.

A server approached with a tray of drinks and Ian took two flutes of champagne. After handing one to Petra, he lifted his glass. "We need to begin this evening with a toast to all of you. Because of our team— our family—we have dismantled one of the largest criminal organizations in the world. Cheers to you," he said and sipped.

"Cheers!"

"But before we begin our meal and really celebrate, I have some news. As many, or rather all of you know, I plan to make some changes." Ian wasn't sure if it was his imagination or not, but to him the room seemed to grow colder and quieter than before. "There are some people we need to welcome to our family, and to others, we need to say goodbye.

"First, allow me to welcome Luis Martinez, formerly of the Denver Police Department. And Marcus Jones, newly retired from the FBI. Both gentlemen will be joining us as operatives. I'd also like to welcome a very familiar face, Petra Sloane, who will be our new legal counsel.

"And as far as goodbyes. We need to bid farewell to both Katarina and Julia. With Marcus Jones and Luis Martinez, they will be opening a new RMJ office in Cheyenne, Wyoming."

"And what about you?" Roman called out, interrupting Ian's remarks. "Are you staying or going?"

"Me?" Ian laughed. "I'm here, brother—just try and get rid of me."

"So we're not here to end one chapter of Rocky Mountain Justice, but begin another?" Roman asked.

He was exactly right. Ian nodded and, lifting his glass high, said, "That's something we can all drink to. To new chapters."

After taking another sip of champagne, Ian dived back in. "There's something else I need to say— something that is long overdue." He passed his champagne to a nearby waiter and slid his hand into his jacket pocket. He gripped the velvet box and dropped to one knee.

"Petra Sloane," he said, reaching for her hand, "will you marry me?"

He took out the ring box and lifted the lid. The diamond sparkled in the light.

"Oh, Ian," she said. Her eyes sparkled as much as the ring. "It's beautiful."

"Is that a yes?"

"Yes," she said. "Yes! Yes!"

He placed the ring on her finger, and finally, he felt whole. "I can't wait to spend the rest of my life with you, Petra."

"I thought our lives were beginning today."

It was the perfect thing for her to say.

"You need to kiss her," Roman called out, teasing.

Ian stood and wrapped Petra in his embrace. His lips met hers and the room filled with a cheer.

Petra ended the kiss, smiling and wiping at her eyes. "I don't want a big wedding. Something small and intimate, with our closest friends and family."

Ian swallowed. Now it was the time for him to actually be nervous. "I have a date in mind," he said. "What do you think about now?"

Petra's expression burst into a huge smile. "There's nothing I'd rather do more than be your wife."

* * * * *

*Don't miss the previous books
in Jennifer D. Bokal's
Rocky Mountain Justice miniseries:*

Her Rocky Mountain Hero
Her Rocky Mountain Defender

*Available wherever Harlequin Romantic Suspense
books and ebooks are sold.*

SPECIAL EXCERPT FROM

H HARLEQUIN®

ROMANTIC suspense

*When Elissa Yorian first met K-9 cop Doug Murran,
she never expected she'd need his professional help.
But as soon as someone attacks her, Doug is on the case,
and he's having a hard time not making it personal.*

*Read on for a sneak preview of the next book
in the K-9 Ranch Rescue miniseries,*
Trained to Protect
by Linda O. Johnston.

"I just wish I had some idea who it is, and why."

"Yeah, me, too." Doug had a sudden urge to take Elissa into his arms, hold her tightly against him, maybe attempt to cheer her a little by kissing that alluring yet sad mouth of hers…

But of course he wouldn't do that. Never mind that he felt attracted to her, or that he wanted to fix things for her. He had plenty of reasons not to get involved with her other than as a civilian who needed help. But she did happen to be a civilian who needed help.

A vision of his uncle Cy's face flashed in his mind, encouraging him and Maisie to become cops like him— and to act like professionals at all times.

"Anyway," she said, "I'll be working at my local hospital tomorrow and Sunday, both as a nurse and doing therapy dog work, so I won't be home much this weekend. Then I'll head back up to Chance on Monday to give my first therapy dog training class. I'll call you then and maybe we can catch up on what's going on here and there."

HRSEXP0918

"All right," Doug conceded. What else could he do? He might be concerned about this attractive, dog-loving civilian, but he wasn't even a cop in the jurisdiction where she lived who could theoretically give her orders—or at least conduct some of those patrols and drop in on her sometimes.

And he clearly wasn't convincing her to do something else—except to walk her dog along with a neighbor. Some of the time. Without additional protection at night.

"Well, be sure to keep in touch." He recognized that his words had come out in a tone of command, which appeared somehow to amuse her.

He wanted to kiss that smile right off her lovely face... but didn't.

He motioned for Hooper to join him at the door, where he removed his dog's leash from his pocket and snapped it on his collar. "Let's go," he told his well-trained partner.

Peace also came to the door to see them off. While they stood there, Elissa petted both dogs. Then, to his surprise, she leaned toward him. "Drive carefully," she said, and planted a soft and swift kiss on his lips before backing away. "And I can't thank you enough for all your help."

You just did, he thought, but all he said was, "You're welcome. Be careful, keep in touch, and we'll see you next week."

Need an adrenaline rush from nail-biting tales
(and irresistible males)?

Check out **Harlequin Intrigue®**
and **Harlequin® Romantic Suspense** books!

New books available every month!

CONNECT WITH US AT:

Facebook.com/groups/HarlequinConnection

Facebook.com/HarlequinBooks

Twitter.com/HarlequinBooks

Instagram.com/HarlequinBooks

Pinterest.com/HarlequinBooks

ReaderService.com

**ROMANCE WHEN
YOU NEED IT**

SGENRE2018